HEART OF TEXAS

DEBBIE K MEDLIN

WestBow Press books may be ordered through booksellers or by contacting:

WestBow Press
A Division of Thomas Nelson & Zondervan
1663 Liberty Drive
Bloomington, IN 47403
www.westbowpress.com
844-714-3454

ISBN: 978-1-6642-5219-6 (sc)
ISBN: 978-1-6642-5218-9 (e)

Print information available on the last page.

WestBow Press rev. date: 1/12/2022

To my five granddaughters
Whose talents, aspirations and accomplishments
Inspire me

Imagine for a moment that your house, the four walls that surround you, would cheer you on, witness your cries of joy and see your tears of defeat. Or could even hear your prayers of praise or anguish. What would your house say about your life and the deep secrets you thought no one else knew?

Come meet the Bailey family who lived in Oak Hill, a small town located on the outskirts of Austin, Texas, during 1918 through 1933, a most turbulent and remarkably innovative time in Texas history.

The door is wide open, waiting for you.

CONTENTS

THE OLD HOUSE

JULY 2005

The bright July sun glared down unmercifully on the gravel driveway leading from the road to the old house. Shimmers of sunlight skipped and bounced across the hot pebbles. Scrub brush and blackberry vines along the road had grown up over the fence long ago, hiding its tall, rickety planks. The old paint-stripped mailbox near the road's edge, the only visible landmark.

The two-story white limestone house, surrounded by elm, oak, cedar, and juniper trees, sat serenely under the Texas sky. Columns, constructed of limestone, supported the overhang of the second floor and extended from the porch steps. Intact, but needing paint, decorative wooden posts and railings encompassed both stories. Three gabled windows jutted out from the rooftop. On either side, two massive smokestacks towered over the roof's edge. Large windows evenly spaced around the entire house beckoned sunlight and offered breathtaking views of the hillside.

From where I sit, I have a good view of the rolling hillside for miles around and especially the long gravel driveway as it enters from the road. Occasionally, I hear vehicles as they pass by to and from town. There are so few who travel that old dirt farm road anymore. Seems they'd rather use the highway. I don't have many visitors. Sometimes curiosity seekers pull in, but don't stay long.

It is another hot day, but I'll wait patiently for their arrival. They always come, or at least one of them comes, about this same time every year. They never all come at the same time. It's sad how we drifted apart. I never knew why or what happened to keep them away.

What's that? I hear something. Is it a car? Is it turning in? Yes, yes! Oh, they're here! They're here!

A bronze minivan stopped in the circular driveway. Six people got out. A man, three women, and two children stood on the gravel driveway, admiring the house. The man walked across the steppingstones leading to the porch. Tall blades of grass and dandelion weeds smothered many stones from view.

Wildflowers—black-eyed Susan, bluebonnets, pink primrose, and orange Indian paintbrush— bloomed in the flower beds by the front steps. The plants crowded and pushed against each other as if a floral competition were underway. The winner would proclaim the prize for the most colorful blooms and densest foliage. Ivy, honeysuckle, blue morning glory, and red trumpet vines snaked intermittently around the six-foot trellises along the east and west side porches.

The man walked up the six porch steps. He glanced at the wicker swing hanging in front of the tall, double windows on the east end. Several wooden rocking chairs lined either side of the entrance. The massive oak door held slender panes of stained-glass panels on both sides. He turned his key into the lock and jiggled the knob. He pushed against the door with his shoulder.

Turning to his family, he said, "Come in, it's open."

The others followed him eagerly into the brightly lit foyer.

"It's so good to be here again. She's something, isn't she?"

The six visitors stood in the spacious entrance hall, observing the slightly dusty floors and the cobwebs clinging like well-crafted silk puzzles from one corner of the room. The red oak staircase, an artistic display, stood straight ahead on the right. The vertical balusters, or rails, were shaped like slender vases. Pomegranate flowers and English ivy leaves were beautifully designed and flawlessly carved down their sides. The handrails were smooth and the steps wide. Tall, fluted newel posts stood on either side of the first step.

A stepdown to the right side of the entrance hall led into the formal sitting area. The room could have easily been encased in a museum—antique furniture, majestic Queen Anne chairs, a rose-colored brocade sofa with tufted seat cushions. An upright piano set against the wall and a grandfather clock constructed of reddish-brown pecan wood stood in one corner. Several large round rugs, some gold others green, were scattered about the light oakwood floor. Beige crocheted doilies were placed on the side arms of the chairs.

This room, even this house, to some might seem like stepping from a time machine capsule or looking through a reversible mirror into the past, but to Frank Bailey it was home.

Frank busily opened the front windows in the parlor that stretched almost to the ceiling. Mary, his wife, flipped on the ceiling fan switch, hoping to stir any kind of breeze. Stuart, ten-years-old and full of curiosity as most boys his age, lifted the cover from the piano keyboard. He rubbed his fingers lightly over the keys. He pressed down the middle "C," extending his fingers to play a chord. The piano plinked ever so softly. His six-year-old sister, Lizzy, gazed intently at the framed photographs displayed across the top of the piano. The frames posed on a crocheted runner, its long, fringed ends draping over each side.

"Is it true, Grandpa? Were you born in this house?" Lizzy, turning to face her grandfather, brushed her soft brunette curls away from her sweaty forehead with the back of her hand.

"Not me, sweetheart. My father was. Aunt Lucy was. Here, Aunt Lucy, sit here." Frank held the hand of the eldest woman—hair streaked with gray wisps of wisdom, shoulders stooped from age, skin thin and wrinkled, eyes bright, mind sharp but most often forgetful. Mary quickly removed the coverlet from a chair allowing Aunt Lucy to gingerly lower herself and sit down.

Francesca—the children's mother, nicknamed Frankie—took a seat on the sofa by the front window next to her parents. Lizzy, cradling a framed photo in her arms, crawled into her grandfather's lap.

"Can we look in the picture box Mama told me about, Grandpa?" Lizzy's big brown eyes twinkled as she lifted her head and displayed her sweetest smile.

Frank put his arms around his granddaughter, pulling her closer. He glanced at his daughter who smiled back, raising her eyebrows inquisitively, awaiting his answer.

"Well, baby, I'm not sure where that old trunk is," Frank answered.

"Well, I sure do!" Aunt Lucy exclaimed, waving her hand upwards toward the ceiling.

"It's upstairs at the foot of the bed in the first room to the left."

"Okay, it's probably cooler down here since all of the windows are open. Stu, come help bring it down," Frank said, patting his grandson's shoulder.

Stuart charged up ten steps, stopping briefly on the landing to stare at the stained-glass oval window. Sunlight, reflecting a rainbow of colors, danced over his face as he raced to the top. He leaned over the railing, pretending to fall, and made funny faces at Lizzy. She shrugged apathetically.

"Frankie and I will bring in the ice chest from the van. Anyone want a cold drink?" Mary asked.

"Ooh! I do! I do!" Lizzy said excitedly, jumping up and down, her ponytail bouncing side to side.

"Me, too!" Stuart yelled from the top of the stairway.

Lizzy stayed behind in the parlor. She glanced at her great aunt, who sat with her hands folded in her lap; her chin almost touching her chest. Lizzy smiled as her aunt softly snored. Aunt Lucy fondly called these catnaps and professed every person needed at least nine a day.

Lizzy kicked off her red flip-flops in the corner. She lifted the faded brocade scarf from the back of a Queen Anne chair and wrapped it around her shoulders. She stepped into the foyer by the stairs and twirled around and around as if she were a music box dancer. With her head tilted slightly, she closed her eyes, spreading her arms out as she spun.

Feeling dizzy, Lizzy fell to the floor on the large oval rug at the base of the stairs. Giggling, she rolled over and over the length of it.

Lizzy sat up quickly when she heard steps coming back down the stairs. She tiptoed past Aunt Lucy, being careful not to wake her, and returned the scarf to the back of the chair.

"Boy, this thing is heavy, huh, Stu? Thanks for your help," Frank carefully backed down the stairs carrying one end of the trunk and most of its weight. Stuart followed carrying the other.

Lizzy followed the procession into the parlor, watching as Frank and Stuart gently placed the trunk in front of the coffee table. The box's hinges, once shiny as brass, were rusted and its handles were tarnished.

"Let's wait for the ladies," Frank said, rubbing his hands together to clear away the dust. Motes circled above his head and drifted toward the ceiling.

Mary and Frankie carried in the cooler and placed it on the gold rug in front of the closed double doors leading to another room. As quickly as his grandmother opened the lid, Stuart plopped his hands into the cold ice, retrieving a Sunkist. Lizzy hurried over and pulled out a can of Nehi Grape. Stuart shook his dripping hands like a wet dog shakes its body after a bath. The water sprayed both Lizzy and his grandmother.

Lizzy laughed, plunging her hands into the melting ice, mocking her brother's actions. Startled, Aunt Lucy awoke from the sound of the children's laughter.

"Here, now!" Mary exclaimed. "I'll get a towel from the kitchen to dry this floor."

"Stop that, Lizzy! Mom, the kids will do that. Stu, you both know better!" Frankie scolded her children as she pointed down the hall.

Stuart and Lizzy snickered as water droplets fell from their hands to the floor. They ran down the hallway, wiping their hands on each other's backs. Lizzy stopped at an arched doorway on her right and stepped inside. A long, cherry wood table lined with twelve chairs sat in the center of the room. Above it hung a chandelier of sunlight-reflecting glass baubles. A wooden cabinet filled with elegant rose-trimmed dinner plates and stemmed glasses sat on a faded red-wine colored rug. Lizzy could envision laughter, bright sparkles of reflected light from the chandelier, big dinner parties and tinkling of delicate glassware. Stuart yanked her arm and pulled her back into the hall.

The children pushed open a swinging door and entered the kitchen. While Stuart rummaged through cabinet drawers in search of a towel, Lizzy walked around a large worktable. She rubbed her fingers over the smooth pink stone top as she encircled the table. While Stuart continued his quest, Lizzy pushed back through the swinging door into the hall. Turning to her right, she saw two closed doors on her left: one on the right and one at the end of the hall. She skipped down the length of the hall and turned the glass knob on the closed door. As she opened the door, Stuart slammed through the kitchen's swinging door waving a towel like a whirlybird over his head.

"I found a towel! Hey, what's in there?"

"It's a stairway. Look," Lizzy pointed to the narrow passageway leading to the second floor.

"Stairs in a closet? That's weird!"

"Stuart, where are you two?" Frankie called from the foyer.

Lizzy closed the door and raced her brother down the hall toward their mother. Frankie, clearly annoyed, stood with her arms crossed watching as the children dried the floor.

Completing their task, the children knelt in front of the old trunk, scooting up closer to their grandfather. Frankie and Mary, sipping Diet Cokes, sat on the sofa with their bare feet curled up between them. Frank opened the dome-shaped lid exposing the rose-colored satin lining. The smell of musty cedar filled the air. A mirror, outlined with faded red ribbons, was glued to the center of the lid. Old photos, letters, Christmas cards and yellowed newspaper clippings filled the box. Frank fanned through a few pictures and several cards then held up an 8" x 10" portrait in a dark oak frame.

"This was the last family portrait taken—right, Aunt Lucy? I remember Dad telling me. It must have been taken in the early '30s. Look, you and Aunt Loraine are just girls." He gently dusted the frame with his hand before turning it around for the children and Aunt Lucy to see.

Frank turned the portrait back around and held it facing him. He gazed at the faces of the Bailey family, his family—his grandparents, his dad, his aunts, and his uncles—all nicely dressed, some sitting, others standing, some smiling widely, some donning only half-smiles, others without any facial expressions at all. All were staring straight ahead, staring back at him.

"Tell us about them, Grandpa," Lizzy said as she wiggled into his lap.

THE THOMPSON PLACE

Summer 1918

Oh, so many, many wonderful memories. Well, I suppose, I'm best suited to tell their story. I know the family better than anyone in this county, maybe even this entire state and Texas is a big state! Anyway, for me, their story begins July 1918 when Franklin and Maggie moved to the old Thompson's place on the hill.

Turning off the dirt road, Franklin tried steering the Chevrolet 490 truck away from a deep pothole that set smack dab in the center of the driveway. The back tire caught the edge of the hole and the truck heaved forward with a jolt. Maggie, sitting next to the door, grabbed Samuel, their five-year-old son who was sitting in her lap. She braced him safely against her with one arm and clutched her side, wincing as she jostled to and fro. John, age nine, and Art, age seven, chuckled as they bounced about on the boxes stacked in the bed of the open short-bed truck. Franklin glanced over his shoulder, watching the two boys through the small oval window in the panel behind his head.

Franklin stopped the black truck in front of the house, stepped out and swiped at the dust on his pants with his hat. Samuel scrambled off Maggie's lap and stood on the seat next to her. She adjusted her straw hat, retying the blue ribbons under her chin and smoothed her dress over her knees. She shaded her eyes from the sun as she gazed through the dirty windshield.

Franklin walked around to Maggie's side of the truck as John and Art scrambled over the sides. John, a tall lad with dark wavy hair, cradled a cardboard box in his hands.

"Let me hold 'em, now," Art demanded, trying to snatch the box John held high over his head.

"They're my marbles, Art. Get away!" John pushed Art roughly to one side.

"Some are mine!" Art jumped toward the box as John repositioned himself.

"Boys, stop your fussin'," Maggie called, stepping down from the truck.

Art raced ahead to the big wrap-around porch. Maggie turned and scooped Samuel from the front seat. He wrapped his legs around her. His soft blonde curls tickled her face.

"Oh, Maggie, you shouldn't lift him! He's too big and heavy. You're having our baby! Did you forget?" Franklin retrieved Samuel from his wife.

"How could I?" She laughed as she patted her swollen belly.

Maggie leaned back against the truck as the life within her kicked under her ribs.

"John, come back for your little brother!" Franklin swept Sam up on his shoulders, waiting for John to retrieve his youngest brother.

"Stay close to the house," Maggie commanded. "Sammy, stay with your brothers."

"We will, Mama," John replied, taking Sammy by the hand.

The boys walk-ran toward the house where Art was impatiently waiting for them on the porch. Sammy's short legs churned to keep up with his eldest brother. John and Art continued their quarrel over the marbles as they ran into the house with Samuel tagging behind.

Franklin wrapped his arm around his wife's shoulders.

"Maggie," he said softly. "Welcome home!"

Maggie looked at her husband through pooling tears.

"Oh, Franklin, this is more than I ever dreamed. I knew the Thompson's place was for sale; everyone in town was talking about it. It's really ours? How could you keep this a secret?" Maggie asked, teasingly poking Franklin's ribs.

"It was hard, believe me! I wanted to bring you out here a dozen times. Nice surprise?"

"It's so big! So beautiful! I don't know what to say." She took a step forward, losing her footing on a loose stone, and stumbled backyard.

"Maggie! Be careful!" Franklin took her hand, steadying her as they walked up the walkway to the porch.

"Oh, Maggie, you should have had a house after Sammy was born. Five years was too long to expect you and the boys to live in those three tiny rooms above the drugstore."

"Franklin, I told you a long time ago, eleven years to be exact, that I would follow you anywhere. Remember? That meant living in boarding houses when we first married and then living above the store. How else would we have gotten our business started?"

"Well, we did save money, didn't we? When this place came on the market, I couldn't refuse. Thompson's niece who lives in Boston didn't want the house or any of the furnishings. Was glad to get rid of it, it seems."

"Hard to believe she didn't want any of this. It's so beautiful!"

"Yeah, she just wanted the land to lease out. She sold us twenty acres along with the house."

"What about the furniture and dishes your mother gave us, Franklin?"

"Fred and Jim brought those in from Jim's barn this morning. Anything you don't want, we can sell. I think this will be a perfect place to raise our boys."

"This may be our little girl, Franklin," Maggie said, holding his hand over her stomach.

Franklin smiled, pulling her hand up, kissing it softly.

"What took you so long?" Fred Jeter teasingly called from the porch. "Jim and I stacked most of the boxes in the area by the stairs. Need to know where you want them. There's still some furniture in my wagon around back."

"Fred, I appreciate your help today. I couldn't have done this without you both. You're good neighbors and better friends. Thanks."

"No thanks needed, Franklin," Fred replied. "You'd do the same for one of us."

"I'll help unload the furniture as soon as I show my wife her new home."

As they entered the house, Franklin held Maggie's hand, watching her eyes survey the details of every room—the walls of the entrance hall were aligned with pegs to hold coats or hats; the foyer displayed a red oak wood staircase of exquisite craftmanship; the stained-glass oval window above the first landing of the stairwell was breathtaking. They peered into the parlor with tall windows covered with white Chantilly lace curtains. The room to the left of the entrance boasted a white marble fireplace. Its mantle was intricately carved with almond flower blossoms and swirling scrolls. A large ornate oak desk sat in front of two windows sheathed in red velvet drapes. There were two more spacious rooms further down the hall on the left. On their right, an archway led to the dining room. A picturesque candle chandelier hung over a long, cherry wood table.

Franklin held Maggie's hand tightly as he led her further down the hallway. Their steps echoed across the wood floor as they walked.

"The back stairs is through that door," he pointed to the end of the hall. "There are six rooms upstairs and four of them open out onto a veranda. There are outside stairs by the back porch leading to the second story. Three more rooms are in the loft. We should have enough space in the shed behind the barn for extra storage. There's even a small stone cottage near the barn. I don't know its condition. The barn and corral could use a little repair. I was thinking about raising chickens, or maybe a few goats, or having a couple of horses for the boys to ride. What do you think?"

Franklin searched Maggie's green eyes; she remained silent but nodded.

"There is an old orchard out back and a plat that looks like it may at one time been a garden. I know how you love gardening. A washhouse sits a few yards from the back of the house. I'll build a new clothesline. I'll show you all that later. This is the room I want you to see."

Franklin pushed open the swinging door to the kitchen and stepped aside for Maggie to enter. She gasped and asked to sit down. Franklin hurriedly pulled out one of the eight chairs from the rectangular-shaped table under the double windows. As Maggie sat, she glanced out at the trellis covered with blue morning glories. She looked around the kitchen at the cupboards that stretched the breadth of three walls. A large wood cook stove and an ice box sat parallel to a tall worktable in the center of the room. A row of coal oil lamps waiting to be filled sat on the cabinet.

"Maggie, here's the pantry," Franklin said, opening the door wide enough for her to see. "Enough shelves here for all of your canned fruits and vegetables this winter. There's a mudroom off the back porch through the door there. A pipe runs from the windmill by the corral to a pump in the mudroom. The boys can wash up and leave their shoes by the back door. That should help keep the floors clean, right? Maggie?" Franklin asked, eagerly. "Maggie?"

Maggie had uttered very few words since entering the house. She leaned onto the table, folded her head onto her arms, and sobbed.

"Oh, darling, don't cry," Franklin knelt by his wife and put his arms around her.

She lifted her head and pulled her husband's face to hers. She kissed him once, then once more. "I don't think I've ever been as happy as...," Maggie began.

John and Art blasted in from the mudroom. Their bare feet were covered in mud and their pants were soaked to their knees.

"Mama! Papa!" John cried, breathlessly.

"Let me tell them," Art blurted.

"No, I will. I'm the oldest," John insisted, pushing Art aside.

"Tell us what? Where's your brother?" Maggie asked, fearfully.

"We were wading in the creek and...," Art said, ignoring his brother.

Maggie abruptly stood to her feet, "Where is Samuel?"

Franklin squeezed the top of her shoulder. Samuel peeked around the corner of the door, then walked slowly into the room. He was wet from head to toe. His curly blonde hair was plastered to his forehead, and his face could hardly contain his smile.

"Here, Mama," he answered.

Maggie sat as Samuel crawled onto her lap. She kissed his forehead, his nose, his cheeks, and his mouth repeatedly as he giggled.

"Sam, Sam," she said with each kiss. "What would I do if something had happened to you?"

He wrapped his legs around her as best he could, beaming after each kiss.

"Are you boys okay?" she looked up at her two older sons, pulling at their arms to bring them closer. She tucked her hand under Art's chin to inspect his face. His mousy-blonde hair was wet, and his blue eyes sparkled with excitement. She kissed his nose.

"We were in the shallows, Mama. The water wasn't all that deep, but Samuel wanted to lie in it," John said, brushing his dark hair from his hazel eyes. Maggie slipped her arm around him listening intently.

"Then he started splashing us!" Art interrupted.

"But that's not what we wanted to tell you! We saw fish in the creek. Could be catfish! Can we go fishing, Papa?" John asked, excitedly, pulling away from his mother.

"Oh, is that what this is about?" Maggie asked as Samuel squirmed backwards off her lap. "Are you boys trying to get your father out of working?"

Maggie took off her hat and placed it on the table. Franklin laughed as he guided the boys back through the mudroom and out onto the back porch.

"Boys, this is a busy day. I promise to take you fishing tomorrow. I know exactly where the fishing gear is packed. Sammy?" Franklin knelt beside his son.

"Yes, sir?" he answered.

"You shouldn't go to the creek by yourself. You must wait for me or your brothers, understand?" Franklin hugged his youngest son tightly.

As he stood, he jostled the tops of John's and Art's heads. He patted them both on the back and said, "For now, go explore this great big yard. Climb some trees, but not too high. Dig in the dirt. Stay out of the way while we unload, okay? And, boys, stay close to the house."

Franklin watched his boys chase each other around a tall elm tree before returning to the house. Using an old towel that hung on a peg near the door, he mopped up the muddy tracks on the mudroom floor. He placed the soiled towel in the sink as he heard Maggie calling him.

"Franklin, come see what Jewel and Letty have brought us!" Maggie exclaimed.

Franklin entered the kitchen as Fred Jeter's wife, Jewel, and Jim Carson's wife, Letty, placed two woven baskets on the worktable.

"Jewel, Letty, thanks for this!" he greeted them warmly.

"Look, Franklin, enough fried chicken, biscuits, jelly, and canned peaches for a week!" Maggie exclaimed, peeking under a red cloth covering one of the baskets.

"Now, maybe not quite that long," Letty laughed. "We knew you two would be too busy to cook with all this unpacking to do. So, we thought we'd bring a few things."

"How can we help you, Maggie?" Jewel asked.

"Oh, I don't know where to begin," Maggie answered. "I'm still in shock."

"I'm so happy for you. Moving couldn't have come at a better time. Not much longer now, huh?" Jewel asked, hugging Maggie.

"No," Maggie rubbed her stomach, "just a week or two."

"Well, ladies, if you'll excuse me," Franklin said as the women continued to chat.

Franklin tried getting Maggie's attention, but she was too preoccupied with her friends' conversation to notice him. He smiled, shrugged his shoulders, and exited through the mudroom.

"Did you read in the *Gazette* the right for women to vote was killed in the Senate?" Letty asked, as she pulled an apron over her head and tied the strings around her waist.

"Again? Unbelievable," Maggie answered. "Guess that means Alice Paul will be getting a women's march together somewhere. I'm sure we'll read all about that, too. Remember five years ago the day before President Wilson's inauguration when she organized the parade of eight thousand women? They marched with banners and rode floats down Pennsylvania Avenue to the White House. What was it the President said to them?"

"Not yet time to amend the Constitution!" Letty answered.

"What about only last year when she was in jail for seven months and refused to eat? Fortunately, newspaper articles about her treatment in jail prompted her release and created support for our cause," Jewel added. "What will it be like to be able to vote alongside our husbands?"

"A miracle I'd say! Want to help unload those boxes over there?" Maggie asked.

"You just tell us what you want done, Maggie. There's no need for you to tire yourself," Jewel said, pushing the heavy box across the floor to the worktable.

"Or hurt yourself," Letty added. "I'll make some lemonade from the lemons we brought. I brought a pitcher and glasses. Didn't think you'd have yours unpacked, yet."

"Oh, lemonade sounds so good. It was a hot, dusty ride in from town. The potholes were unbearable! I thought I'd have this baby before we got to the house!" Maggie laughed.

Maggie ran her hand over the smooth surface of the pink-red colored granite countertop on the worktable. "This is stunning!" she exclaimed.

"Fred told me this house was built sometime in the late 1880s using white limestone from the Oak Hill quarry and this granite from Granite Mountain in Marble Falls. Both were used at the State Capitol. Have you seen it?" Jewel asked.

"No, sadly I have not," Maggie answered.

"Did you see the latest Sears, Roebuck Catalog? Hemlines are coming up to mid-calf," Jewel said, changing the subject. "Corsets are still suggested, but I don't know why. Thankfully, I don't wear one!"

"Ha! A corset! Would take an enormous amount of boning and fasteners to bind this stomach! I don't care how short the hemlines get as long as I get out of this boxy thing," Maggie laughed as she flapped the large collar of her blue gingham dress.

The women laughed as Jewel took a plate from the box. She held it up, turning the white plate over, admiring the red roses trimming the edges.

"Those were Bessie's, my mother-in-law's," Maggie said. "We didn't have china when we married. Since she had several sets, Mama Bailey let me choose a couple. She was relieved; it was fewer things to pack and move."

"She's living in Oklahoma, right?" Jewel asked.

"Yes," Maggie answered. "I think I've told you when Franklin was in college, his father died unexpectedly. So tragic. My heart ached for them. Still does. Something you just never get over. Franklin offered to quit school and take care of his mother and Lorna, his sister, but Mama Bailey completely refused. She was invited by her aunt and uncle to come to Boise City. So, Mama Bailey and Lorna moved to Oklahoma instead. Lorna now has two girls, Susan, five and Claudia three." She unpacked another plate. "Anyway, Lorna married six years ago when she was only seventeen. It was all I could do to keep Franklin from bristling off to Oklahoma and bring them back to Texas. He thought Lorna should go to college, and that Wilson was far too old for her. Mama Bailey was convinced he was a good Christian man so that was that."

"How old was he?" Letty asked as she stirred sugar cubes into the lemonade.

"He was twenty-seven when they married. His first wife, Kaye, died six months before. He had two boys. Alexander was eight and Gavin five when they married. Lorna loves them dearly, but Alex still resents her and gives her a hard time."

The women continued to talk, sip lemonade, and laugh as they unpacked boxes.

It didn't take long for the Baileys to set up housekeeping at the old Thompson's place and call it their own.

WILLIAM FRANKLIN

SUMMER *** FALL 1918

Franklin rushed through the front doorway, Jim Carson at his heels. They were halted to a stand-still by Matilda Lawrence, Doc Lawrence's wife. She stood in the middle of the foyer. Her hands poised on her hips like a school marm waiting to scold a disobedient child.

Letty Carson stepped up from the parlor and took her husband's arm. Franklin glanced into the room. Fred Jeter was pacing in front of the grandfather clock, drinking a cup of coffee. Fred tipped his head in Franklin's direction.

"Franklin, you finally made it!" Matilda Lawrence grabbed Franklin's arm and practically pulled him upstairs. "Good thing Jim found you when he did."

"Is Maggie okay? Is anything wrong?" Franklin asked. "And the baby?"

"Oh, Maggie's doing fine. Doc's with her. No baby, yet, but it'll be any time now. You're as jittery as a new father. Look at you! You'd think this was your first!" Matilda, a robust woman of fifty-five, chuckled as they ascended the stairs.

"Well, Matilda, this is my first 'fourth' child," Franklin said, irritably.

Matilda patted his arm and smiled, "The boys are up in John's room with Jewel. They'll be glad to see you."

As Franklin stepped across the threshold of John's room, his three sons rushed to greet him. Samuel hung onto his legs; John and Art clung to his waist.

"Now, now, boys. Everything is okay," Franklin reassured his children.

"Where's mama?" Samuel cried, holding tightly to his wooden airplane.

"Oh, Sammy, your mama's having our baby today," Franklin said, kneeling in front of his youngest son. "You're going to be someone's big brother! Jewel, why don't you take them to the kitchen for something to eat? I'll join you later, boys. Okay?"

Franklin waited until Jewel and the boys were descending the stairs before he turned toward his and Maggie's bedroom. He tapped softly on the door.

"Doc?" he called.

The door opened and Doc Lawrence, a tall fifty-eight-year-old man, receding hairline and paunchy stomach, slipped out. He closed the door behind him and rolled down his shirt sleeves. He extended his hand to shake Franklin's.

"You may see her soon, Franklin. She's doing fine. I'll tell her you are here."

"Thanks, Doc."

"Now, don't worry. I've done this a time or two and so has Maggie. I'll call for you soon. Would you mind asking Matilda to join me?"

"Are you sure everything's okay?" Franklin asked, anxiously.

"Yes, yes, Franklin. I just like her help, that's all. It's all right," Doc patted Franklin's shoulder before going back into the room and closing the door.

Franklin came back downstairs. His friends were standing in the foyer, studying him closely as he descended the stairs.

"Doc needs you, Matilda," Franklin said.

"Fine. Franklin, you look a fright. Letty, take him to the kitchen. Have you had lunch?" Mrs. Lawrence asked.

"We'll take care of him, Matilda," Letty answered. Taking Franklin by the arm, she led him to the kitchen.

After eating a bowl of tomato soup, crumbled high with cornbread, Franklin watched his boys who were sitting on the floor playing with their wooden tops. John, leaning against the worktable, worked his top effortlessly. Art attempted to show Samuel the artful skill of spinning, but as hard as he tried, Samuel's top only wobbled.

Fred brought in a stack of chopped wood and placed it in the wood box by the stove. He poured himself another cup of coffee and leaned against the cabinet to drink it. Jewel and Letty busied themselves around the kitchen, washing dishes and sweeping the floor. Jim brought in a bucket of water from the mudroom. Letty dipped several ladles-full of water into the kettle to heat on the stove.

Franklin stood and joined Fred for a cup of coffee. After taking the bucket back to the mudroom, Jim poured himself a cup and joined the men.

"Cotton prices are increasing to twenty-six cents per pound. That's one good thing about this war, may be the only thing. It doesn't hurt that we Texas farmers have the Houston Ship Channel to export our cotton. How long has it been? Wasn't it just last April, almost a year now since President Wilson asked Congress to declare war against Germany? I've reserved several acres for wheat and corn following Hoover's food-conservation program," Jim said. "Not fond of the meatless Tuesdays and porkless Thursdays and Saturdays but Letty follows those rules to a tee."

"I've planted corn, too. Jewel has added more vegetables to her garden and started a canning club. "Hooverizing" is an odd nickname for the program, but we're doing our bit," Fred answered. "I noticed you've placed a "Buy More Bonds" poster in your drugstore window, Franklin."

Franklin nodded as he took a swig of coffee.

"Have you registered with the National Registrar?" Jim asked and both men nodded.

"At least I know now you're no older than forty-five. Guess I'm too old, but only by a few years!" Jim scoffed "Didn't your son turn eighteen this year, Fred?"

"Yeah, David registers in August. I'll tell you one thing; his mama is not keen on this Selective Service Act and this whole conscription idea. We're praying this war in Europe ends soon before either of our numbers are drawn," Fred answered.

"I read in the paper that the U.S Army Signal Corps completed construction of several training fields and schools for aviators in Texas cities. San Antonio, Waco, and Houston to name a few. Thanks for coming today. I sure appreciate you both," Franklin clapped Fred on the back and returned to his spot at the table by his boys.

"You can't spin a top! You're a baby! Want your mama, little boy?" Art taunted, snatching the top from his brother. "You're a mama's baby!"

"Am not!" Samuel argued, his face turning red.

"Are, too! Baby, little baby. Babies suck their thumbs!"

Mrs. Lawrence pushed open the kitchen door breaking up the argument. The room fell as silent as a prayer as she walked to Franklin's side. He looked up, anxiously.

"There's someone upstairs who would like to meet you," she said, cheerfully.

The boys scrambled to their feet. Franklin hoisted Samuel up onto his shoulder. John and Art fell into place on either side of their father as they hastily departed.

"I sure could use a cup of tea," Mrs. Lawrence said, walking briskly to the stove.

The Jeters and the Carsons waited impatiently for Matilda Lawrence to pour the steaming water over the tea-leaf strainer balanced on her cup. No one dared ask about the newest addition to the Bailey family. Knowing Matilda would stay mum even if asked, they, too, remained silent, and exchanged quizzical glances.

When Franklin knocked on his bedroom door, Doc Lawrence opened it widely. He smiled, excused himself, and left the room. Franklin stood in the doorway as if in a trance, still holding Samuel on his shoulder. John and Art stood like miniature statues under his elbows.

Maggie sat in bed propped against three pillows. Her long brunette hair cascaded over her shoulders. She wore a white dressing gown trimmed in lace. Crooked in her arm, she held a bundle tightly wrapped in a white blanket. A pastel yellow coverlet lay smoothly over her legs.

"Come in," she smiled, patting the coverlet beside her. "Boys, come meet your brother, William Franklin. Come in. It's okay, you'll have to move away from the door, Franklin."

Franklin swung Samuel down from his shoulders and the boy ran to his mother. He hoisted himself upon the bed, but the mattress was too high. He struggled, losing his balance after two attempts. John picked him up and sat him on the end of the bed. Samuel crawled over to his mother. He fell across her legs, holding on tightly as if she might evaporate. Maggie stroked his curly blonde hair. Franklin leaned over to kiss her.

"Sammy, come here, sweetie," she whispered.

Maggie handed the baby to Franklin. She pulled Samuel up, holding him tightly against her chest. With his legs straddled around her, she rocked him side to side. He peered up at her and smiled as he snuggled closer. He turned his head so his brothers could not see and began sucking his thumb.

Franklin eased down on the side of the bed. John and Art sat beside him. Franklin pulled the blanket down from the baby's face. Tears welled in his eyes. John and Art stared at this new creature sleeping in their father's hands.

"God is good, Maggie. The baby is perfect. You're beautiful," Franklin stood to kiss his wife once more. "William Franklin, a fine name. A fine baby boy," he added.

After several minutes of silence except for Maggie's humming to Samuel, Franklin asked John to invite everyone downstairs to come up. The older boys raced down the stairs. Sammy held tightly to his mother as if aware the tiny being in his father's hands would soon be his replacement. Shortly the sound of excited voices could be heard spilling down the hallway.

Excitedly, Letty and Jewel followed the boys into the room. Fred and Jim lingered in the hallway. Franklin stood and handed the baby to Letty. She held William, softly cooing at him.

Jewel rushed to Maggie's side and squeezed her hand. "Maggie, Doc will be back up in a minute, but we have to get back. Sue Ellen has been with the other kids all day. I'm sure she'd like to be rescued. There's stew on the stove, chopped wood in the box, and the lamps have been filled. Fred will bring fresh eggs in the morning."

"Oh, thank you, Jewel. Thanks to you all. You're such dear friends," Maggie said, tearfully.

"Oh my, seems ages since mine were this little," Letty said, handing the baby to Jewel. "We have to go, too. Now, if you need anything, Franklin, we're just down the road."

"We'll be fine, Letty. Thank you for today," Franklin said.

He joined the men in the hallway. Jim and Fred took turns shaking his hand, clapping him on the back, and extending offers for any additional help.

Franklin nodded, a loss for words.

Four months later, Franklin came home late one evening after a three-day trip to San Antonio to attend a conference and to pick up medical supplies at the San Antonio Drug Company. The house was dark and quiet as was to be expected for the late hour. He slipped quietly up the stairs. He checked on John and then Art, both sleeping soundly in their rooms. The small room joined by a common door to Franklin's and Maggie's was perfect for a nursery.

But for now, it was Samuel's. Franklin readjusted the blue blanket tangled around Samuel's legs.

Franklin closed Samuel's door softly. Entering his room, he adjusted his eyes to the darkness. He glimpsed toward the bed. The blanket was pulled up over the pillows, but Maggie was not there. He looked about and smiled. She sat in a rocking chair in front of the opened double doors leading out to the veranda. The moonlight poured through the doorway casting light on her bare feet. Franklin tiptoed across the floor and stood beside the chair. Maggie was asleep, her head crooked to one side. William was asleep, nuzzled at her bare breast.

Franklin knelt beside her. She looked so beautiful there in the moonshine. Her face so serene, so peaceful. With the back of his thumb, he traced the top of his son's forehead down to his tiny nose. At Franklin's touch, the baby began to suckle earnestly even as he slept. Startled, Maggie opened her eyes.

"He's asleep," she whispered, readjusting the baby in her arms.

"So are you, darlin'," he smiled at her, caressing her cheek. He leaned forward placing a soft kiss on her lips. "Here, give him to me. Go to bed."

"He will wake if you move him too much."

"Maggie, he's sound asleep. Surely, I can lay him in his cradle. Go on now." He gently took the baby from her and steered her toward the bed.

"Okay, I'm so tired. Sammy wouldn't sleep in his bed and stayed cuddled next to me for hours. When he finally fell asleep, I carried him to his bed. He's getting so heavy. The baby will be awake again in a couple of hours," she mumbled, sleepily.

"I want to tell you about my trip. There're plans for a retail warehouse to be built closer to Oak Hill, so I won't need to go so far for supplies."

"Wonderful, tell me all about it tomorrow." She brushed his lips with a kiss before quickly slipping under the bed covers.

After rocking William in the cradle at the foot of their bed to assure he was asleep, Franklin undressed. He crawled into bed. Moving closer to his wife, he wrapped his arm around her waist. He leaned up on his elbow and twirled a lock of her curled hair around his finger.

"Maggie?" he whispered into her ear, pulling her close. He kissed her shoulder, yearning to make up for three days away. "Maggie?"

She was sound asleep.

"Sleep well, my sweet," he whispered, pulling the coverlet around her shoulders.

Such good news, Franklin! You've worked so hard as a health advocate for this community. Your fourteen-month course of instruction at the College of Pharmacy in Galveston has certainly proven beneficial. Must be a relief to know you can keep your shelves filled with quinine imported from France, opium, morphine, raw ginger, cod liver oil, Radway's Ready Relief and all the other compounds, ointments and salves your drugstore requires.

Medicine is in such high demand now with this new strain of influenza. Who knows how long it will last? What are they calling it? The Spanish flu? Oh, yes, I recall your reading the newspaper article to Maggie about a local doctor downplaying the disease, claiming there was no cause for alarm. But that wasn't the case, was it? Hundreds of Austinites as well as people all over the world have died. An outbreak was reported in two army camps, too. Camp Travis in San Antonio and Camp Logan in Houston. People who do get sick are quarantined and treated with quinine or aspirin to reduce fever. The Texas Board of Health warned city and county officials to be vigilant about protecting the civilian population. Austin's Mayor Woolridge with the approval of the council members and city attorney shut down Austin last month for thirty days. The university, public schools, churches, movie houses, businesses, and other places where people assembled were closed. Oak Hill followed Austin's lead. Maggie turned the library into a schoolroom. The boys, silly things, grumbled about missing their friends and having to stay home. But I didn't mind. Maggie along with Letty and Jewel and other women from church made masks at home to donate to the cause. Everyone wears a mask outside their home these days. Even you, Franklin. The war and now this! What a trying time! When will it end?

One afternoon in early November, Maggie was in the washhouse doing laundry. Using a wooden dowel rod, she scooped up a shirt from the hot, soapy washtub and placed the tip of the rod at the center of two wringer rollers. The wringer with a crank attached to one side was situated between two tubs—one contained sudsy water the other clear. After placing the dowel rod to one side, she turned the crank with one hand. With the other she gently guided the shirt between the rollers to the other side. She watched as the garment squeezed through the rollers and plopped into the clean hot water. Clean clothes—wrung several times to remove excess soap or water—sat in one bucket ready to hang on the clothesline outside to dry. Dirty clothes sat piled in another bucket. Her dress sleeves were rolled up over her elbows; her face and arms sweaty from the steam escaping from the washtubs.

"Maggie!" Franklin, excitement in his voice, stepped unexpectedly through the doorway.

Startled, Maggie looked up from the washtub, and lifted her apron to wipe her face. The look on Franklin's face was alarming. "What's wrong? Why are you here in the middle of the day?"

Franklin pulled around a newspaper he'd been holding behind his back and held it up. In broad letters across the frontpage Maggie read, "WAR IS OVER! GERMANY HAS SURRENDERED!"

"A Special Edition paper was thrown against the door of the drugstore. I couldn't wait until tonight to share the news. The article also says, oh, here, I'll read it, 'Germany has surrendered to the Allies this day November 11, 1918. A cease fire has resounded ending all fighting. A Special Edition issue will be printed Thanksgiving Day, November 17th, to recount President Wilson's address to the nation.'"

Maggie threw her arms around Franklin's neck. "Oh, could this be true? Is the war over?"

Indeed, it was true! Texans served their country well. They say 200,000 Texans served in a variety of military branches and units.

Sadly over 5,000 lost their lives. Celebrations of the war's ending sprung out all over the state. Upon their arrival home, the 36th Infantry Division paraded down the streets of downtown Fort Worth. Such excitement! Every year houses of worship and firehouses would toll their bells at 11:00 a.m. on November 11th to commemorate when all fighting ceased…the 11th hour of the 11th day of the 11th month.

I remember Franklin reading from the newspaper part of President Wilson's address that Thanksgiving. Wilson said, 'It has long been our custom to turn in the autumn of the year in praise and thanksgiving to Almighty God for His many blessings and mercies to us as a nation. This year we have special and moving cause to be grateful and to rejoice. God has in His good pleasure given us peace. It has not come as a mere cessation of arms, a relief from the stain and tragedy of war. It has come as a great triumph of Right.'"

Is this truly the war to end all wars as they say?

Oh, and I must also tell you the Spanish Flu which came in three waves finally waned in 1919 almost as quickly as it began. Funny thing about its name…Spanish Flu. The disease did not originate in Spain as you might think. During the War, the press in neutral Spain tracked the infection's progress in their newspapers unlike the newspapers in the warring nations that censored theirs. Hospitals treating the sick, mortuaries burying the dead, grocery stores providing food, drugstores dispensing medicine, warehouses and other businesses were overburdened with the effects of the influenza epidemic.

The Spanish Flu was the greatest avalanche of death since the Black Death, or bubonic plague, that struck Europe during the mid-1300s. It's also reported this influenza, the Spanish Flu, killed millions of people around the world. More, in fact, than were killed during the Great War. This epidemic was particularly infectious and dangerous for healthy adults aged twenty to forty. Almost every family, worldwide, dealt with this devastating influenza in some way or the other.

I'm hopeful we won't face this type of disease or catastrophe ever again!

GUESTS

Spring 1919

Maggie swept a loose curl from her face as she broke eggs into a black cast-iron skillet and tossed the shells in a small bowl. Crispy bacon, stacked neatly on a platter, was warming near the stove. Biscuits were browning in the oven. The boys sat at the table patiently waiting for breakfast or as patiently as young hungry boys can possibly wait. William, now eight months old, sat in his wooden playpen in the corner of the kitchen chewing on the end of his blanket. Franklin, adjusting his tie, came bounding down the back stairs and greeted his family.

"Morning," he kissed Maggie on the back of her neck. "John, go down to the road and bring in the mail and the newspaper from the mailbox, please."

John scooted his chair back and rushed from the room. Art fiddled with his spoon spinning it lengthwise to see how fast it could spin. Sammy, his elbows propped on the table, looked on mesmerized. William began to fuss.

John burst into the kitchen. "Papa! Come see who's here!"

Maggie and Franklin exchanged glances. "Who could it be this early, Franklin?"

Franklin left the kitchen with John close behind. Maggie shook her head at the other two scrambling from their seats, discouraging them to follow. She picked up William and straddled him on her hip.

Franklin entered the kitchen, looked warily at Maggie, and stepped to one side. A tall, handsome, thin-framed man, wearing a worn, blue-striped suit stood in the doorway, hat in hand.

"Ernie!" Maggie gasped as she handed the baby to Franklin and embraced her brother tightly. "Why didn't you tell us you were coming?"

Ernie pulled back, holding her shoulders, and looked at her. "You are beautiful, still, baby sister. Franklin's taking good care of you!"

"Ernest! You've always been a tease. You look a sight. When did you eat last? Oh, sorry, I sound like Mother! Tell me the latest. Where have you been? Why haven't you written? Franklin, let's move to the dining room where there's more room."

"Maggie, wait," Ernie stepped into the hall and led a young girl, who looked no older than eighteen, into the room. "I'm pleased to introduce Suzie Bond, my wife."

Maggie, clearly shocked, just stared at the girl. The girl's dark-blonde hair, plaited on both sides, made her look even younger. The braids fell over her shoulders from beneath her felt hat. Her frock was faded and oversized, concealing her upcoming motherhood, but not that well. Franklin placed William in his playpen and invited Ernie and Suzie to the dining room. Maggie placed the platter of bacon and biscuits and a bowl of scrambled eggs on the blue tablecloth covering the table. She gathered plates, cups, saucers and utensils from the china cabinet and placed them around the table.

"Boys, take your places and let's eat breakfast," Maggie ushered the boys to their seats and returned for the baby.

After Franklin gave thanks, conversation seemed stifled and awkward. Ernie was introducing his older nephews to Suzie. She didn't speak, only smiled weakly, her uneasiness painfully obvious. Ernie always had a knack of cracking jokes and making others feel at ease. The boys were boisterous, laughing at their uncle's stories, clearly delighted by his visit. Franklin, too, tried to fill in the gaps of silence by talking about new building projects, the new cotton gin, the town and how it was growing. William sat pacified in Maggie's lap as she gently bounced him. Ernie's charm, this time, did not appease his sister. She focused upon keeping her composure, but her mind was reeling with questions.

William began to squirm and cry. "If you'll excuse me, please," Maggie said as she stood and lifted William to her hip. "I need to tend to the baby."

"Of course," Franklin replied. "We'll take care of this. Boys, if you're finished eating, take your plates to the kitchen. Then you may go outside to play. John, take Sammy's plate and watch out for him."

Maggie hurried down the hall eager to escape to the room where the piano was housed. She was relieved to have a hungry baby as an excuse. She sat in the gold tufted Queen Anne chair and removed her apron. She laid it over the arm of the chair as the baby continued to voice his displeasure. She held William tightly with one hand as he squirmed. She unbuttoned her dress quickly and untied the ribbon on her chemise with the other. He was impatiently straining against her, his little face red from crying. Cooing at him, she settled him toward her gently. She pulled the lace chemise to one side. He suckled hungrily. She wiped at the tears that were running down his nose. William held tightly to her fingers before she could withdraw them from his face and watched her intently.

A soft knock was heard on the door. Maggie grabbed the apron and placed it over her shoulder, covering herself. Ernie cracked the door asking if he could enter.

"Yes," Maggie replied, smoothing the apron over the baby.

"May I?" he asked, pulling an upholstered ottoman closer to where Maggie sat. He patted her knee and sat back. "Suzie is helping Franklin with the kitchen. I must explain. Before you start with questions, I know what you're going to ask. You need to know about Suzie. You and I have always been so close. I'm so sorry, Maggie, that I didn't write or send a telegram. It all happened so fast…no, that's not fair. Suzie deserves more than that."

Ernie paused for Maggie's reaction, but she remained silent, hurt, and silent.

"I met Suzie last year in Wichita Falls working with a construction crew on a bridge project. I made a fair amount of money. Well at least enough money for train tickets here and some left over. The project was going well. Suzie is my crew chief's daughter. She was around the site all the time, coming sometimes after school to see her father. I was invited to their house for dinner, and Suzie and I had an instant connection. She was so bubbly, as cute as a bug's ear, and seemed captivated by my every word. Then she began coming around the site to see me. We started seeing each other with her parents' blessings, of course. I was flattered such a pretty, enthusiastic, sweet young lady would be awe-struck by an ole bloke like me. You do think she's pretty, don't you?"

Maggie nodded, "But she's so young, Ernie! You're thirty-one! How old is she?"

"Eighteen her next birthday. But she looks older, don't you think? It's my fault for getting involved too fast. I fell head over heels. She is just so adorable and lovable. When she said she was in the family way, her father insisted we marry." Ernie rubbed his hands through his hair. "I would have anyway without his threats. I will do right by her. You know I'll care for this baby. I'm to be a father! Amazing, isn't it? I haven't told Mom or Dad either, but I will. Afraid they'd be disappointed in me, as always. I never wanted to follow in Dad's footsteps and be a farmer. But never mind that. Suzie and I absolutely love each other, Maggie, honest."

Ernie reached out. Maggie removed her hand from under the apron and grasped her brother's hand. He clasped it tightly as tears edged his eyes.

"When is she due? Where are you living? Do you have a job?" Maggie hurled question after question.

Ernie grinned. "Always the mother-hen. She's due in a couple of months, I think. There's a project in Austin I heard about and hoped we could stay here until I earn enough for us to find a place of our own. It won't be long. I promise!"

Maggie's mind tumbled like a tumbleweed rolling across an empty wind-swept field. Two babies plus three children under the age of ten; two more adults to feed plus all the extra cleaning, cooking and laundry. She looked at her older brother, who for the first time she ever remembered, seemed so lost and unsure of himself.

"I'll speak to Franklin."

So, at Ernest's insistence John and Art did not need to share a room as Maggie suggested. He and Suzie settled into the small room, Maggie's sewing room, adjacent to the mudroom. It was spacious enough for a bed, dresser, rocking chair, and baby cradle. Ernie argued that with his long hours, early departures, and late arrivals from work, plus a newborn, the room would be perfect. It was easily accessible through the back door and since it was on the lower floor, the family upstairs wouldn't be disturbed.

Owen Randall Bond was born one month later to the day—a tiny little thing, long legs and arms, weighing a mere six pounds. Suzie's hard labor lasted one full day and most of the night. Dr. Lawrence reported afterwards both she and the baby were fine and healthy.

Suzie did not take naturally or joyfully to motherhood. She left the baby in his cradle until she could no longer tolerate his crying. Maggie tried to encourage her and help with the baby's needs, but Suzie didn't appreciate advice or assistance. After six weeks, Suzie became sullen and reclusive, only coming from her room to eat. Then during meals, only speaking when directly addressed. Ernie, too, tried to console her when she would sometimes cry in her pillow. She would either pull away or flinch at his touch. Often, on Sundays, his day off, their arguments and her crying, as well as Owen's, seeped through the thin walls.

One night when Ernie came home, the Bailey household experienced a misfortunate tragedy that carried with it immeasurable consequences.

"Franklin?" Ernie called softly, lifting the coal lamp, as he waited in the doorway for an invitation to enter. "Franklin?"

Maggie sat up abruptly as Ernie edged the door wider with the toe of his boot.

"Ernie, what's the matter?" Maggie asked, jostling her husband awake.

"She's gone!"

"Who's gone?" Franklin asked, sitting up.

Maggie rose and pulled a shawl over her nightgown.

Ernie began pacing, "It's late…I know. I'm sorry. I came home and found Owen sound asleep in his cradle, but Suzie was not in our room. I looked in all the rooms downstairs. She's gone! My God! What will I do? Where can she be?"

Maggie hugged her brother, trying to console him. Franklin slipped on his trousers, pulled his suspenders over his night shirt, and stuffed his feet into his boots.

"We'll find her, Ernie. Don't worry. She's probably out on the porch or down by the garden," Maggie encouraged.

Franklin grabbed the top of Ernie's shoulder. "Take my truck and go to the train station, just in case. See if she's there. I'll look around the barn and the yards. We'll find her, Ernie. Maggie, should you check on Owen?"

Maggie hurried down the back stairs. Before entering the room, she could hear the baby's whimper, a kitten's mewling. She placed a lit coal lamp on the dresser and peered over into the cradle. Owen had kicked off his blanket. Maggie lifted him from the cradle. His gown was soaked through. She laid him on the bed to change his diaper and gown. His cries became persistently louder, his lungs quite strong for such a slight body.

"Oh, there, there," she cooed, kissing his tiny face, as she wrapped him in a blanket to warm him. The warmth did little to soothe him. His cries increased. Maggie sat in the rocking chair, loosened her nightgown over her shoulder, and coaxed the infant to nurse. After a few tries, he latched on and began to suckle. "That's better, isn't it, little one? We'll find your mama, don't worry, sweet thing."

Owen stared up at her, his eyes watching, concentrating, as if trying to recognize the person holding him. Finally, relaxing his taut body, he closed his dark eyes, fully contented. As Maggie rocked her nephew, she patted his bottom and rubbed his legs. She hummed a lullaby as she lovingly gazed at him.

"Where's your mama, little one? Oh, Suzie, where are you? Who could abandon their baby? Dear Lord, help Ernie find this precious child's mother."

At sunrise, Suzie was still missing. Franklin and Ernie had not yet returned. Everyone was so anxious, so worried! What's to be done?

Maggie busied about the kitchen making breakfast for her boys. John and Art were old enough to assume what was happening and did not ask questions. Earlier, she and John brought Owen's cradle into the kitchen to be closer to them. Owen, his tummy full once again, was sound asleep. The sounds of clinking and clanging in the kitchen or the chattering and playful racket from his four cousins did not disturb his peaceful slumber.

As the boys finished eating oatmeal and toast, Franklin walked into the kitchen looking weary and discouraged. Maggie, who was spoon feeding oatmeal to William as he sat on her lap, looked up expectantly. Franklin shook his head slowly. The boys gathered around as he sat at his place at the table. He ruffled their hair and sent them outside promising to join them after he had eaten.

"Any word?" Maggie asked.

"No, Ernie is still at the station. The night ticket agent had gone home before he arrived, and Ernie is trying to find any information the day agent may provide. He's desperate. I stopped by Fred's and Jewel's. Fred is bringing Sue Ellen over later to help you with the children." Franklin reached across the table and squeezed Maggie's hand. "If anything were to happen to you, or if I could never find you, I don't know how or if I'd survive!"

Maggie lifted William and placed him on her hip. She put her right arm around her husband's shoulders and kissed the top of his head. "I would never leave you, my love."

Franklin slipped his arm around her waist and leaned into her. William reached out with oatmeal-covered fingers, grabbed his father's hair and pulled. Franklin and Maggie laughed as she stepped back.

"Breakfast is on the stove and the baby is sleeping. I need to bathe and feed this one," Maggie said, as she kissed William's fingers. "You'll be okay with Owen? He should be good for another two hours."

Franklin nodded and stood to get his breakfast.

That evening Franklin heated water on the wood-burning stove in the kitchen for the boys' baths. Maggie gathered them into the library for story time, a regular weekday routine. It was Art's turn to read. He had selected "The Tale of Peter Rabbit." They crowded onto the sofa in front of the bookshelves. John and Art sat on either side of their mother. Sammy stood, squeezed between John and Maggie, to better see the illustrations. William was asleep lying against Maggie's shoulder. Owen was asleep in his cradle at her feet. John held the book while Art read and turned the pages.

"Maggie, Ernie is here," Franklin announced entering the room. "Come on, boys, the tub is ready. Sammy, you can be first." He lifted Sammy from the sofa.

"What about Peter Rabbit?" Sammy asked demanding Franklin's undivided attention.

"Sure, why not? Art, bring the book. You can read while I scrub ole Sammy here." Franklin tickled his son, throwing him over his shoulder. "Come on, John. Maggie, I'll get this crew to bed. Ernie is getting a cup of coffee and a sandwich first. Then he'll join you."

Maggie laid William down on the sofa and covered him with a blue patchwork quilt. Curled on his knees, William slept with his buttocks in the air and his thumb in his mouth. She peeked at Owen who was still sleeping soundly. The baby lay on his back with his arms resting by his head, his little hands formed into fists. He looked so peaceful unaware of what chaos filled the world about him. She pulled his blanket under his chin and stood to smooth the wrinkles from her dress, anxiously waiting for Ernie.

As Ernie entered the room, Maggie rushed toward him embracing him tightly. She kissed him and led him to a chair. Maggie pulled up another chair and sat with her knees touching his. He leaned closer and took her hands.

"Mag-gie," he cleared his throat and began again, "Maggie, I'm leaving on the first train out in the morning. After I described Suzie, the station agent said a young girl fitting her description bought a one-way ticket to Wichita Falls. I'm going to find her and bring her back. This afternoon I hired a wet nurse for Owen, a Mrs. Foster. I paid her a month's wages upfront. She had only one condition... that she's off Saturday nights after 8:00 through Monday morning at 6:00. On Sundays, she wants to be home with her three children and her mother who live in town. I don't know anything else about her except what Reverend Collins shared that she's trustworthy and loves babies. Jewel had suggested to Franklin that Reverend Collins might help. Mrs. Foster will be here in the morning to meet you and will return the money if her terms are not agreeable. Maggie, oh Maggie, I'm asking so much of you. I'll make it up somehow. I promise!"

Ernie leaned back, covered his face with his hands and wept. Maggie had only seen one other man cry before...Franklin when his father died.

Why do men think it unacceptable to show emotion? It grieved Maggie so to see her brother in such distress. Two distraught souls.

Maggie hugged Ernie, trying to comfort him. "We'll do whatever you need," she said softly.

At the sound of Owen's stirring, Ernie wiped his eyes with the back of his hand. He stood and knelt beside his son's cradle. He lifted the baby carefully and held him in the crook of his arm.

"My boy," he whispered over and over. "My baby boy."

"Ernie, it's time to take our babies to bed."

She lifted William from the sofa, wrapping the quilt around him, and followed Ernie upstairs.

The arrangement was mutually agreed upon between Maggie and Mrs. Foster. Since she had no mode of transportation, Mrs. Foster's brother, Ralph, who also lived in town and owned the icehouse, picked her up every Saturday evening after work. He dropped her off every Monday morning before his morning ice deliveries.

Franklin asked Fred and Jim to help move a bed and chest from the shed to one of the spare rooms upstairs. Maggie couldn't imagine Mrs. Foster staying in the small room adjacent to the mudroom. She prepared one of the more spacious rooms with doors that opened out onto the veranda. Better accommodations would keep Mrs. Foster more comfortable.

Within the three months Ernie was away, the two women bonded easily as they sat on the veranda rocking their babies, sharing stories about each other and their families. Maggie relished the company. Mrs. Foster, Elizabeth, was a most genteel, soft-spoken, outgoing person. Also, a hard worker, she was willing to help with any household chore.

Mrs. Foster's story was indeed a sad one, poor dear. She and her three children moved to Oak Hill from Port Arthur, Texas, to live with her mother after her husband died in 1915. He was a crewmember on the Gulflight, a tanker owned by Gulf Refining Company. The tanker departed Port Arthur April 10, 1915, carrying 56,000 barrels of gasoline to a port in France. The U.S. had stayed out of the war in Europe during this time and being neutral was allowed to trade with both the Allied and Axis powers. Two British patrol vessels suspected the tanker was seeking to refuel German submarines operating in the vicinity and escorted the tanker to port for examination. Germany had different ideas about neutrality, it seems. The tanker was torpedoed on May 1st by a German submarine. The tanker was heavily damaged off the Isles of Scilly, near the southwest coast of Great Britain. Two men on the crew drowned, one being Elizabeth Foster's husband of fifteen years. The Gulflight was the first American vessel to be torpedoed during the Great War.

Elizabeth's two older children, Anne and Dottie, were now fourteen and ten; her youngest, Harold, was five. For extra money to help support her family, Elizabeth Foster became a wet nurse after Harold was weaned. Owen was her third charge.

Ernie did not find Suzie in Wichita Falls. After hours of pleading and coaxing, more for Owen's sake than his own, Suzie's mother finally gave in. Suzie was in Arkansas living with her eldest son. When confronted in Arkansas, Suzie, persuaded mostly by her brother, was adamant about not returning to Texas and most insistent upon ending their marriage. Astonishingly, she also gave up legal rights to Owen. An attorney was hired, documents prepared, signed by both parties, and witnessed by her brother and the court clerk. Ernie returned to Oak Hill more depressed and heart-stricken than when he left.

Ernie was employed by a construction crew building a warehouse near Williamson Creek. In his spare time, he renovated the stone cottage behind the barn hoping one day to make it his and Owen's. Until then, he lived in the small room he and Suzie had shared. Life goes on nonetheless, but it must be extremely difficult to embrace tragedy and heartbreak and keep going. One day at a time, one breath at a time, I often heard Ernie say.

One rainy late afternoon when work on the warehouse had been postponed and progress on the cottage impossible, Ernie shook the rain from his hat and pulled off his rain-soaked boots in the mudroom. He smelled a strong aroma of coffee coming from the kitchen. He pulled on dry boots and hurried in hoping to visit with Maggie. Elizabeth Foster was bathing Owen in a tin tub in the sink. At six months, Owen had been sitting up fairly well on his own. But as a precaution, Elizabeth balanced him against the side. She laughed as he splashed and kicked the water with his hands and feet.

"Oh, sorry," Ernie, clearly embarrassed, turned to leave.

"Mr. Bond, no need to be embarrassed. This is your son. Come bathe him." She held out a bar of soap wrapped in a washcloth.

Ernie's face reddened more deeply as he took the soap. "I've not bathed him before."

"It's simple."

"He's so small."

"Nonsense. Here, roll up your sleeves and give me your hand."

Without consent or refusal, Elizabeth hardly waited until his sleeves were rolled before taking his hand and plunging it under the warm water. She held his wrist and spouted instructions to rub the soap on the cloth. Standing so close to her, Ernie was uncomfortable. Her hair smelled of honeysuckle and her hands were soft but firm. Owen splashed even harder as Ernie rubbed the soapy cloth over his baby's chest and back, arms and legs. One big splash caused Ernie to jump back quickly.

Elizabeth smiled, "You'll get the hang of it with more practice. Here, I'll finish. There's coffee on the stove."

Ernie poured coffee into a large mug and sat at the table to watch Elizabeth finish bathing his son. He watched attentively as she leaned toward the baby and made silly faces and goo-goo sounds. Ernie hadn't noticed her jovial side before, how laughter brightened her eyes. Owen squealed with delight. She rinsed the soap from the baby's body and lifted him up against her, caring less that she was getting wet. Talking and cooing at the baby, she laid him in the center of a towel stretched out on the counter and wrapped him snuggly like a caterpillar in its cocoon. She walked to Ernie's side and held Owen out to him.

"Here, kiss him goodnight. I'll retire soon, too. The veranda and a good book are calling my name."

Ernie took his son, kissed his face and handed the precious bundle back to Elizabeth.

"Good night, Mrs. Foster."

"It's Elizabeth. Good night, Ernest."

The kitchen carried the usual din of sounds around the breakfast table. John, Art, and Sammy sat on one side of the table eating biscuits, bacon and fried eggs. The older two were chattering about the first day of school. Sammy, moping because he was still too young to go, pushed his eggs around his plate with his fork. The baby boys, each tied into the highchairs Ernie had built for them, sat with Maggie on one side, Elizabeth the other. The babies ate every other bite of oatmeal offered them, clearly distracted by the boys. Franklin used the last bite of biscuit to sop up the egg yolk on his plate. He chewed quickly as he pulled his watch from his pocket to check the time.

"If you'll excuse me," Elizabeth said, untying Owen from his chair. "I think I'll take Owen out before his morning nap to see his dad. Ernie must be hungry since he didn't join us for breakfast." She reached across the table and wrapped the last biscuit in her cloth napkin. She balanced Owen on one hip and left through the mudroom.

"Boys, it's time to go," Franklin announced returning his chained watch to his vest pocket. Maggie immediately stood to grab for John as he came around the table. She took a brush from her apron pocket and brushed his hair vigorously. At first, he pulled back, then gave in, knowing this was not a battle he could win.

"There, my handsome boy. Have a good day," Maggie whispered. John thinking ten years of age too old for kisses, pulled away before his mom could embarrass him further.

Art came up behind and hugged Maggie around the waist. She turned and patted his cheek, "Need to go over the times tables one more time?"

"No, Ma'am, I know it."

Maggie hugged him tightly. "Yes, you do! Go on then."

"Boys, get in the truck. I'm right behind you." Franklin motioned for Maggie to follow.

"Sammy, come sit by Willie, please," Maggie commanded.

Sammy grinned as he scooted into the chair once occupied by his mother and began playing "keep-away." Sammy leaned as close as he dared before Willie could reach out and grab his nose. Both giggled at the near misses.

Maggie followed Franklin down the hall to the front door. He stopped abruptly and she collided into him. He turned toward her with a mischievous smirk. "Don't tell me you haven't noticed?"

"Noticed what, Franklin?"

"Elizabeth and Ernie. 'Oh, my, Ernie missed breakfast!'" Franklin chimed in a sing-song voice. "I think she spends as much time at the cottage as he. Using Owen for an excuse, really? It's so obvious."

"Why, Franklin Bailey, you should join the Ladies Quilting Circle with as much gossip as you conspire. And they say women are gossipers!" Maggie smiled as Franklin's blue eyes twinkled mischievously.

Franklin laughed as he kissed Maggie's forehead. "Mark my words, my pet. There's something in the air."

"Oh, go to work, you romantic!" Maggie kissed his cheek.

Elizabeth heard sounds coming from the barn as she approached. Ernie had turned a corner of the barn into a make-shift carpentry area while repairing the cottage. The barn doors on either end were widely opened to provide air. Ernie, shirtless, braced one knee across the wood plank as he sawed using deep, even strokes. His arm muscles flexed with every movement. He looked up when Owen squealed. He grabbed his shirt off a railing and quickly pulled it over his head. He had no idea how long Elizabeth had been standing there but was pleased she was. Elizabeth extended the napkin toward him. He graciously took it and his son from her.

"Breakfast. I saved the last one. Your nephews are big eaters."

"Yes, they are. Thank you. Hello, big man!" He placed the napkin on the unsawn plank and lifted his son up over his head. Owen squealed and kicked the air with his chubby legs as Ernie lifted him again.

He balanced Owen on his hip as he opened the napkin to retrieve the warm biscuit. Owen reached out for the bread forcing Ernie to turn his head and gobble it down in three bites.

"So, Maggie tells me Anne turns fifteen tomorrow," Ernie said, wiping crumbs from his mouth.

"Yes, she does, and I'll save you the trouble from asking your next question. You must be curious. I'm thirty-six," she smiled coyly.

Alarmed, Ernie stared at her in disbelief for never would he have asked her age, nor did age matter. But he had to admit this fine-looking, full-bodied woman standing before him made him feel nervous and perplexed.

"Um, no, that wasn't my next question. I was going to ask if I may take you home on Saturday evenings. No need for Ralph to come all the way out here to pick you up. Would that be acceptable?"

Without answering she patted her hands together and extended her arms out to Owen. The baby reached for her. She took Owen, brushing her hand against Ernie's arm. She placed Owen on her hip and gazed into Ernie's eyes. Smiling she turned toward the barndoor.

Looking back over her shoulder, she said, "That would be nice, Ernie. I'd like that."

So, it was no surprise to anyone in Oak Hill, especially Franklin and Maggie, when Ernest and Elizabeth married two months after Owen's first birthday. A beautiful fall wedding, it was. Ernest bought the small home that Elizabeth and her mother were renting in town with aspirations of adding on to accommodate their growing family. Elizabeth's children loved Ernest instantly. Elizabeth's mother moved in with her son, Ralph, and was so thankful that her daughter was once again married to a caring, hard-working man. She was pleased, too, that her daughter and her grandchildren were noticeably happy.

Maggie was extremely happy her brother had found a woman who dearly loved him. She knew their devotion to each other would make a nurturing home for their blended families. She missed Elizabeth's company, of course. With the babies both weaned, she knew Elizabeth would have had to eventually leave. Marrying Ernest was the perfect scenario as now Elizabeth was family.

What did surprise Franklin, however, was Maggie's announcement that she was once again with child. Clayton Stuart was born in the spring of 1921. Another healthy baby boy. John was now twelve, Art ten, Samuel eight, William three.

The Bailey family was growing by leaps and bounds. Five strapping, growing boys.

PROGRESS AND PEACHES

SPRING 1921

One Sunday morning as the Bailey boys were hurrying out of church, Willie saw a big dog curled at the bottom of the church steps. He tugged against John who was helping him down the steps to the street. Sam and Art quickened their steps to follow.

Willie squealed in delight, "Look! Doggie came to see Jesus!"

Willie pulled and tugged against John's hold as the four boys came down the steps toward the scared animal. Franklin, who was at the top of the stairs talking to the minister, saw them and hurried down.

"Wait! Careful now, boys, I don't know this dog."

The female dog, her coat matted with dirt and grime, lifted her head and watched the boys descend the stairs. She seemed anxious as Willie neared. Art pulled Willie and Sam back just as Franklin darted between his sons and the dog.

"Wait, Willie." Franklin held his hand out. The dog sniffed it and laid her head back down on her paws. "She's so thin. Looks like she's not eaten in a while," Franklin observed.

"Can we keep her, Papa?" Willie asked.

All the boys, including John, echoed Willie's request. Coming out of the church, Maggie saw her husband and children at the base of the steps. Carrying the baby in the crook of her arm, she walked down to investigate. Franklin looked at her as the boys continued to repeat their question. Franklin dared not answer without Maggie's consent. The boys noticed their father glancing at their mother. Suddenly surrounding her, they asked if they could keep the dog. Willie hopped up and down on one foot as he pulled on her skirt. Maggie gently pushed her sons aside and handed Clayton to Franklin. She knelt on the ground beside the dog.

"Oh, dear, what's this? Oh, Franklin the poor thing is starved! Look at her! We must take her home and take care of her."

That's all the boys needed to hear. John picked the dog up carefully and carried her to their truck. Art grabbed Willie's hand and followed Sam as they hurried to keep up. John placed the dog gently in the flat bed of the truck. The boys climbed over the sides. Willie scurried to sit next to the dog, stroked her fur and whispered into her ear. Franklin helped Maggie and the baby into the front seat and headed home.

On their ride home, the boys debated on just the perfect name for their new pet. She was half golden retriever and who could guess what the other half might have been. Her fur under all the dirt seemed a light shade of reddish gold. Finally, after several name suggestions—Red, Girl, Sadie, Lady, Lass—had been mentioned, Willie announced, "Peaches! She looks like peaches."

John and Art laughed. "She does look like a ripe peach, Willie!"

So, the dog was named Peaches.

After food and water and tons of love and attention, Peaches began to perk up. After adding a little weight, she became a beautiful dog. Her hair became soft and glossy, her brown eyes bright and inquisitive. The boys loved her immensely and she followed them everywhere. She seemed to always be hungry; always under foot when Maggie was cooking, clearing off the table, or discarding table scraps.

"You're gonna get fat, my dear." Maggie would say as she held out another piece of bacon or bite of biscuit for Peaches to jump up and gobble.

One weekday afternoon Maggie was in the kitchen ironing. Clayton was asleep in the crib by the window. She returned one iron to the wood stove to heat. As she reached for the second iron that had been heating, Art frantically ran into the room.

"Mama, I can't find Willie!"

Maggie turned to face him, "What?"

"Willie! Mama, he was playing with me and Sam on the rope swing. Then I turned around and he was gone! I've looked upstairs. He's not there!"

Maggie moved both irons away from the heat and took Art by the hand as they walked to the door. "Where is John?" She asked calmly.

"He's looking for him now. Oh, Mama, where could he be? He can't climb up to the tree house by himself! We've looked everywhere!"

As Maggie and Art walked onto the side porch, John came running from the barn.

"Mama, I've looked in the barn, down by the old stone house—I've climbed our favorite tree just in case—I've looked, Mama. I've looked!"

"John," Maggie patted her twelve-year-old son's shoulder. "We'll find him. Don't worry. He couldn't go far, right? He was just with Art and Sam." Art shook his head in agreement.

Sam ran from the other side of the house. His face red and sweaty from running. "I can't find him! Should we get Papa?"

Maggie pulled her apron up to wipe Sam's face. She had to keep her wits about her. It was too far into town to send the boys for Franklin. "Boys, let's think, where could he be? He couldn't be far...oh, and where is Peaches?" She had suddenly noticed Peaches was not underfoot.

The boys looked puzzled. Where was Peaches? While running around as the four of them had all morning, she would be biting playfully at their heels.

"I haven't seen her all day!" John exclaimed.

The boys anxiously called out for Peaches. Their search for Peaches and Willie was taking too long. Panic swept over Maggie like an ivy sneaking up the trellis. She encouraged the boys to keep looking as she slipped into the house to get the baby. Taking two ends of a long piece of soft muslin, Maggie tied them securely at the top of her right shoulder. The excess material formed a pouch similar to an arm sling. Within the pouch she carefully placed Clayton and adjusted the cloth across her chest. The baby slept snuggly against her.

The frenzied search continued. One more time around and if unsuccessful, Maggie knew she must send for Franklin.

As Maggie and Sam neared the front porch steps, Sam grabbed his mother's hand. "Stop! Mama, did you hear something? Was that a dog?"

He quickly ran toward the porch steps and squatted to listen. Hearing no sounds, Sam jumped up and called for Willie as he walked the length of the long porch. He called for Peaches as he turned and walked back the other way toward the steps. Maggie watched him prayerfully hoping that Willie was near. Sam noticed a couple of lattice boards at the base of the house were askew, twisted to one side.

Wooden planks were nailed around the crawl space, the gap between the ground and the house foundation, to keep raccoons or 'possums or skunks out. Although, not always successful. Could Willie possibly be under there?

Sam pulled at the plank with all his might. Maggie called for John and Art. The boys came running from around the side of the house.

"What? Did you find him?" John cried as he knelt beside Sam helping him pull the boards.

"I don't know. I just heard something, that's all," Sam exclaimed.

Maggie wrung her hands as she watched her sons struggling with the boards. She silently began to pray. Finally, the plank gave way allowing a wider space to crawl through.

Art tried to squeeze through, but he was too big. "You'll have to go, Sam."

Sam was small for eight and could easily slip through. Instead, he sat as still as a fence post in front of the opening, staring into the darkness. Everyone knew his hesitation to move was his intense fear of spiders and spider webs.

John and Art coaxed him to try.

Finally, Maggie knelt beside her trembling son and hugged him. "Did you hear Willie under there? You are very brave, Sammy. You can do this. We're right here," she whispered.

Sam looked up at his mother and tried to smile. He looked over his shoulder at his brothers standing behind him. He took a deep breath and scooted on his belly between the boards. Maggie became extremely nervous when Sam slipped completely out of sight. Clayton began to wriggle. Maggie bounced him and patted his back.

John kicked at the dirt. "Papa asked me to mend those boards, Mama. If Willie is under there, it's my fault!"

Maggie put her arm around John's shoulders, comforting him. Art paced back and forth in front of the opening.

Art turned quickly and shouted, "Sam! Are you okay?"

They heard a muffled reply. John and Art agreed to remove more boards and go after Sam, when a little blonde head poked out of the opening. Maggie dropped to her knees as she helped Willie out. She was crying joyful tears as she hugged him tightly. Willie's face and clothes were smudged with dirt; his sweaty hair smelled like wet chicken feathers. She held him too tightly causing Clayton to squirm and cry.

"Help!" Sam's muffled voice was getting closer to the hole. John and Art knelt in front of the opening.

"Over here," John directed, peering into the gap.

Maggie and Willie turned back toward the porch. John stood and turned around to face his mother. He grinned broadly as he held three squirming pups in his arms. Art pulled at Sam's legs guiding his brother backwards. When Sam was clear, he stood and turned to face the others. He was holding two pups. Art looked back into the hole and coaxed Peaches out. Willie wrestled away from Maggie and ran to Peaches. The boys squatted on the ground looking at their dog and her five puppies. Maggie hugged Sam and kissed his dirty, sweaty face. He whispered to her that two pups died. He'd go back later to get them. Now it seemed he had conquered his earlier fears.

"Willie?" Maggie looked at her youngest as he sat with his brothers and the wriggly puppies, three males and two females. "Why did you go under the porch, son?"

While gently stroking one of the little male pups, Willie answered, "Cause Peaches was under there. She's a mama like you! Look!" He held up the pup for his mom to see.

"Yes, I see. Did you not hear us calling for you?"

"Yes, but Peaches and her babies needed me!" he answered matter-of-factly.

"Please, you must answer when you hear us call. We were very worried about you, understand?"

Willie nodded his head as the puppy, eyes still closed, nuzzled up against his chin. Maggie smiled as she patted Peaches' head. She held Clayton to her chest and leaned over to kiss the dog on the nose. "And I thought you were just eating too much!"

She instructed John to carry Peaches into the barn and make a nice bed of hay for her litter.

When the puppies were weaned, the boys were told that they could keep only one and the others would be given nice homes to friends in town. Several people from church had heard about the pups and requested either a male or female. Even Doc Lawrence, whose office was next door to Franklin's drugstore, had asked for a female pup for his daughter, Marilee. Deciding on one pup to keep became an exceedingly difficult task for each of the boys had a favorite. Finally, the older boys determined that Willie should be the one to choose the pup. Without hesitancy and with much eagerness, Willie chose the little male that he had fallen in love with that very first day.

The pup was very playful. He had light golden hair with a big dark brown spot on the end of one of his long silky ears. "This is Tip," Willie announced as he held the pup for all to see. So, Tip became another welcomed addition to the Bailey family.

Several weeks after the pups had found new homes, the Baileys were having breakfast together in the dining room. The boys were talking about the new school year that would be starting in September, only two brief months away. They talked, too, about the new schoolteacher who had moved to town—a Miss Parker. Maggie told them she had yet to meet her. This was Miss Parker's first year to teach, and she would be teaching Sam's class. John teased Sam about his new teacher until Maggie mentioned she'd heard Miss Parker was forming a 4-H club. That really started the boys jabbering and making plans about what kind of animal to raise and show at the county fair.

As the months passed and Clayton began to crawl, Sam was certain that puppies were much better than baby brothers. Willie, however, loved his little brother. Willie packed him everywhere and thought he was the baby's sole caretaker, releasing his charge to Maggie only when Clayton was hungry or soiled.

Willie loved to swing with Clayton on the front porch swing and watch John and Arthur play catch. Peaches and Tip always joined the fun. Tip barked each time the boys threw the ball and darted back and forth between them. Peaches waited patiently. When the opportunity came, she zipped in and retrieved the dropped ball. Carrying the treasure in her mouth, she'd dart away. Tip followed just for the chase. The boys, exasperation in their shouts to stop, chased after them. Most often a failed quest. If dogs could laugh, I know those two were belly laughing.

While his older brothers played catch, Sam played marbles. Kneeling on the porch, he poured out his marbles from a small pouch and arranged them in a circle by size and color. He'd flick a shooting marble at a designated target. Willie laughed many times watching Sam frantically scramble around trying to catch a stray marble before it rolled into the flower bed.

Oh, how I love to watch children play. They have such imaginations, such energy, such innocence, such fun. Their laughter is most contagious.

One evening Franklin and Maggie sat alone on the porch swing. The boys, their prayers said, had been tucked into bed. The baby was finally asleep in his cradle in the parlor. The window was opened slightly so he could be heard when he awoke. Peaches lay curled at Maggie's feet. As Franklin smoked his pipe, she told him about the boys' activities that day and about how the baby was crawling everywhere. She was not sure Clayton would ever learn to walk. Willie's hovering hardly gave Clayton any space. When the baby crawled too far, Willie picked him up and carried him. Franklin smiled and inhaled his pipe. Exhaling, Franklin held the pipe bowl with one hand and reached for Maggie's hand with the other.

"Maggie, I need to talk to you about something." Curious, she waited for him to continue. "I have been asked by several businessmen in town to invest in a local bank. Wouldn't that be great for our town? The Missouri, Kansas and Texas railway system is headquartered in Smithville, just two hours from here. If Oak Hill had a bank, we could possibly assist with funding the railroad and its employees' needs. Perhaps the railway would be more willing to set up a terminal there—maybe even a maintenance center—a roundhouse. Just think of the job opportunities for Smithville and Oak Hill! If men and their families are sent to work on the line, Doc Lawrence and I could start a side business. We'd check on the linemen and help with minor injuries. Regardless, both of our businesses are bound to grow! You're not saying anything..." Franklin hesitated, looking expectantly at his wife.

"You have not stopped to take a breath! This is a lot to consider! Can our town manage more growth? We only have one hotel, the school, a post office, a feed store, the icehouse, the mercantile, the cotton gin, two churches, Doc's office and our drugstore. Is Smithville any bigger? Where would all these railroad people live? And the bank investment? How much money are we talking about?"

"Oh, Maggie, the investment would be whatever amount we contribute. Our annual revenue would be a percentage based upon the amount we invest. We would be stockholders and have a say in how the bank is run. With the railroad expanding and the business it will bring, we could save more for the boys to go to college, if they choose. I know we both hated to see Ernie and Elizabeth sell their home and move to Fredericksburg last year. But to oversee the building of the furniture factory was a tremendous opportunity for him. Since that project's completed, I've asked Ernie to join the investors, move back and build the bank. I've invited him to live with us. I knew you wouldn't mind. Eventually, he could open his own construction company and take bids from Smithville. He'd have more than enough to do."

"Franklin, be reasonable! Elizabeth has three of her own, plus Owen and their baby. Where would we put seven more people? I am stressed enough with our children. I hardly have time for our older boys. I wanted to go back to teaching music this fall, but then the baby came...." Maggie changed the subject quickly hoping Franklin did not detect remorse over having their last child. "Clayton is not even weaned yet. I don't want John, Art, and Sam to give up their rooms. Willie is still young. The cooking—the laundry—the ironing—the gardening—caring for more children—I just don't know." Maggie put her hands over her face. A pin securing her hair tumbled out releasing three stands of wavy brunette hair to fall around her face.

"Oh, Maggie," Franklin pulled her closer and whispered. "I never wanted to add more stress or more work for you. I should have asked first before making plans with Ernie. Elizabeth would help, I know it! Shh, please, don't fret." He pushed her hair away from her face. "What if we hired someone to help with the housework and the boys?" He pulled her chin up to look into her eyes. "Maggie, my Maggie." He kissed her forehead.

"Franklin, I'm sorry. You know that I love our children more than anything in this world and I always want what's best for them. You know, too, that I will agree with anything you want to do. I dearly love my brother and his family. I know Ernie is struggling now going from project to project, moving his family with him. I've been selfish. I will give up my sewing room. We can move the piano out of the music room and make that a bedroom if need be. Art and

Sam can bunk together in the loft. They won't mind. I want John to keep his room. He's old enough not to share. I'll put Willie back in the nursery with Clayton. We'll have enough room. I'm only tired, I guess."

"Maggie, listen, I almost forgot! A Mr. Santiago and his wife came in the store today looking for work. They have traveled from South Texas and seem to be nice people. Ole Mr. Darter has pestered me for years to plant alfalfa on our acreage and start baling hay to sell to him and the other ranchers. I have been thinking about that lately. Mr. Darter has offered to sell us a couple of his horses, too. I don't know if our old gelding would be up to farming. A baler and a new wagon wouldn't cost much. What if I offer Mr. Santiago a job taking care of the garden, clearing out those dormant ten acres and tending the fields? Mrs. Santiago could help you with the household and the boys. What do you think? Maybe, you could start tutoring again or start music lessons like you've always talked about doing."

"Franklin, can you ever concentrate on one project at a time?" She smiled, slipping her arm through his. "I would love to meet the Santiagos. Maybe they could stay in the cottage. Ernie did such a great job renovating it. It is small but should be comfortable enough for two."

Franklin wrapped his arm around his wife. She pushed against the wood flooring with her toe making the swing move. Peaches' tail swished to the rhythm of the swing. The stars blotted the black sky with tiny pinpoints of light. The sounds of the night included the movement of the rickety swing and crickets chirping in the distance. A baby's cry floated through the open window and interrupted the peaceful moment.

Maggie sighed and whispered, "I think someone is hungry."

Franklin squeezed her hand as she stood. Peaches slowly unfurled herself from her comfortable position and followed Maggie inside. Franklin remained on the porch and relit his pipe; his mind filled with dreams and schemes.

THE SANTIAGOS

SUMMER 1921**SPRING 1927

Luis and Delores Santiago, a hard-working couple in their fifties, began their employment with the Bailey's three weeks later. Mr. Santiago spoke only a few words of English, but Mrs. Santiago was fluent. She had learned as a child from her mother who worked as the housekeeper for an orange grove owner in the Valley. Maggie knew some Spanish, but not much. She was relieved to know that Mrs. Santiago understood and spoke English perfectly. Mrs. Santiago insisted on being called by her given name, Delores. Maggie instructed the boys to address them respectfully as Mr. and Mrs. Santiago. Maggie called her Delores, but only when the boys were not present.

Willie had trouble saying "Santiago" and instead called Mr. Santiago Santos. When Maggie corrected him, Mr. Santiago smiled and said, "Okay. Okay, be Santos." Thinking of Willie's struggle with their name, Mrs. Santiago insisted the boys call her "Tia" which is Spanish for aunt. Maggie finally agreed. So, from that day on, Mr. Santiago was Santos and Mrs. Santiago, Tia.

The Santiagos helped clean the small three-room stone house and were extremely proud of their new home. Franklin and Mr. Santiago repaired the barn. They added stalls for Santos's two horses and his little burro named Pico, a small gray furry fellow with big fuzzy ears. Ole Joe, Franklin's gelding, seemed to enjoy the company of the mares, Chica and Azul. Santos was well experienced with horses and farming.

Before long, tall green alfalfa grass covered the once barren acreage. The garden by the house never looked better. Vegetables from the garden—two kinds of beans, black-eyed peas, corn, squash, melons, okra, peppers, tomatoes, onions and three kinds of potatoes—were always plentiful. Franklin bought a few chickens and a dairy cow, providing a surplus of milk and eggs.

Tip was fascinated with Glo, our cow. He'd creep through the grass and bite at her swishing tail as he ran past. Finally, he stopped when one day Glo kicked him. She must have been tired of being tortured. Served him right, I suppose. Thankfully, he was not hurt. Peaches, however, delighted in chasing the chickens. Art tried desperately to keep her away. When a coop was built, Peaches could no longer chase them and lost all interest in the squawking birds.

Mrs. Santiago loved the boys, and their feelings were mutual. When they helped shell peas on the back porch, she would entertain them by telling stories in Spanish and then interpreting them in English. The boys learned Spanish quickly. They liked to sneak down to the stone house on Sunday afternoons and watch her make tortillas on the stone pit Santos had dug out for her. The boys sat on rocks or tree stumps nearby and waited for their warm, round flat bread. Peaches and Tip ate their fill of bread, too. This became a Sunday tradition for the children for many years.

One Saturday, Tia walked into the kitchen as Maggie was kneading a mound of yeast dough on the worktable. Maggie smiled as she wiped her flour-covered hands on her apron. She huffed at a lock of hair that had fallen across her eyes. Tia dipped two cups of water from the water bucket sitting at the end of the counter and filled the kettle. John was helping Franklin at the drugstore managing the soda fountain and sweeping the floors. After completing their chores, Art and Sam had gone fishing with Santos at the creek. Willie and Clayton were taking a nap.

When the kettle whistled, Tia removed the kettle from the heat. She placed loose tea leaves into a strainer and placed the strainer over the top of a blue ceramic tea pot. She poured hot boiling water into the strainer then turned to face Maggie.

"How long are you going to hide behind that apron?"

Maggie, surprised by her comment, continued to pound the dough and sprinkled in more flour. Tia waited patiently for Maggie to respond. When Tia pushed a cup of brewed tea toward her, Maggie sat down. She wiped her hands on her apron and sighed.

"How did you know? I didn't think I showed," she placed her hand over her middle. "What will I do, Delores? Clayton is only ten months old. Another child! I don't know if…."

Tia reached out for Maggie's hand and held it tightly. "Do not begrudge God's gifts---another baby. Maggie, what could be more perfect?"

"I have not told Franklin, yet. I'm sure he must know. But he has been so busy lately—at the drugstore; or meeting with the bank investors; or making plans for the railroad station and the new windmill in town. Do you think he will be angry? Another child to raise."

"Why would he be, little one? Franklin is a good father, and you are a wonderful mother. Your boys are good boys. God has truly blessed you. Maybe we could have a little girl, no?"

Maggie smiled and squeezed Tia's hand. "A little girl would be nice."

"Mama?" a small voice sounded from the doorway. Willie stood there barefooted. A corner of his shirt stuck out from his pants and his suspender straps straddled his shoulders. He walked over and held out his hands to Maggie. She lifted him onto her lap. He wrapped his legs around her waist and took her face in his little hands. "Are you baking cookies?"

Maggie hugged her four-year-old tightly. "Oh, Willie, yes, we can! Do you want to help?"

Willie patted his hands together as he scooted off her lap onto the floor. Tia winked at her and brought down another bowl from the cupboard. Maggie kissed her son's cheek.

"God's gifts," Tia whispered.

Franklin was delighted when Maggie told him the news that evening on the porch. "We will definitely have to add on to this house, won't we? It's a good thing that Ernie is coming! I hope he brings extra hammers and saws!"

Ernest's family arrived from the Hill Country as planned and his woodworking skills were immediately put to use. The bank building and a barber shop were his first projects. It was not long before he had enough money saved to buy his own land on the west side of town.

During his free time, Ernie worked on the design and the construction of his house. John and Art were eager to help him with any meager task. Maggie loved having her brother close by and dreaded the day when he would once again move his family out. That time seemed so far in the distant future as Ernie was so busy with projects in town.

Elizabeth loved the idea of living with the Baileys again. She insisted that they not be treated as guests and assigned Anne and Dottie household chores. Sam found Harold to be an expert marble player and a new playmate. Maggie felt Elizabeth had enough to do just caring for her own baby, Carter Eugene. But she did appreciate the extra help. The women laughed about being together again under the same roof caring for babies.

Tia did not seem to mind the extra workload either. As she carried a bundle of laundry out to the washhouse, she would chuckle and sing, "So many Niños."

Willie and Owen skipped behind her mocking like little birds, "Niños, Niños."

The railway construction was well underway. Franklin and Doc Lawrence joined ranks to provide medical services for the railway workers. They bought a Ford Model-T to carry their supplies to the line. They set a tent nearby and for a meager fee from the railroad company, they set broken arms and bandaged minor cuts. They provided extra water to prevent dehydration and shade to prevent heat stroke. The railway foremen were appreciative of their services. It kept the workers on site. Sometimes they would stay near the lines for several days at a time. During one of these stays, Patrick Thomas was born.

When Franklin received word to come home, he and Doc Lawrence returned as quickly as they could. The Model-T jolted and bumped over the deep cuts in the road, but finally pulled safely to a stop in the driveway.

Santos met them on the front porch. He slid his straw hat onto his head and smiled, "Más Niños!" He tipped the brim of his hat and made his exit to the barn.

Ernie ran through the front door to greet his brother-in-law and dearest friend.

"They are both fine!" he exclaimed. "Another beautiful baby boy! Tia and Elizabeth helped deliver him, Doc. You need to add them to your staff. We will soon have enough boys to start our own construction business, Franklin!"

On cool evenings, Santos hitched Pico to a small cart that was used for transporting vegetables from the garden. The bottom of the cart was lined with hay then topped with blankets. Led by Santos, Pico pulled the cart to the main house. Willie, Owen, and Clayton were placed on top of the blankets for a ride. Sam walked alongside holding one side of Pico's halter, Harold the other. The little burro pulled the cart and its riders to the barn and back. Maggie and Elizabeth, sitting in rocking chairs, watched from the porch. Anne and Dottie sat on the first porch step and waved each time the cart paraded by. The riders in the cart shouted and shrieked as they tossed hay into the air. Their boisterousness did not seem to bother Pico. The little animal plodded along knowing extra hay waited for him.

The following year, Ernest completed the construction of his house and moved his family to their new home. He leased the empty space next to the drugstore Franklin had acquired three years before. After a few minor remodeling adjustments, Bond's Construction Company was completed and open for business. Bond's Construction was bustling as more businesses opened. Since he was doing so well, Ernie hired more men. He had a proposal to design and build the Methodist Church and a contract for a courthouse on the town square.

The next five years passed quickly for both the Bailey and Bond families. Towns grew quickly with the completion of the railway station in Smithville and with the railroad came more families and more businesses. The 1927 population neared 2,500 in Smithville, over 200 in Oak Hill and over 42,000 in Austin.

LOVE STRUCK

Spring 1927

One new family to come the spring of 1927 was a family by the name of Moore. George Moore became the new manager and editor for a newspaper office in Austin. His wife, Peg, was employed as a 4th grade schoolteacher at Oak Hill Elementary. The Moore's had four daughters—Emily, sixteen, Rachel, fourteen, Evelyn, twelve and Catherine, ten.

Franklin invited the Moores to lunch one Sunday afternoon after church services. He thought their girls would better transition to a new school after meeting his boys. He was certain Peg and Maggie would become close friends. Earlier, Tia had helped prepare roast beef and vegetables from the garden. Afterwards, she retired to her house to spend the afternoon with Santos.

The dining room table was set with the best white lace tablecloth, the silver candle sticks and the blue and white Wedgwood china. Maggie had reminded her sons again for the umpteenth time about their table etiquette and manners. Clayton and Paddy fidgeted as Maggie combed down their cowlicks with the palm of her hand. All the boys were still dressed in their finest Sunday suits and ties awaiting their parents' guests.

When she heard the front bell, Maggie straightened Franklin's tie. They walked to the foyer to greet the Moores. The boys followed in military fashion. They stood by age order—eighteen, sixteen, fourteen, nine, six, and five.

John was extremely indifferent about the afternoon's activities until Miss Emily Moore stepped through the doorway. He readjusted his tie and noticed that Art, too, was smoothing down his vest pockets. John was openly staring at this tall girl with copper curls. She was followed by three younger girls.

He heard his father make introductions, "This is Mr. and Mrs. Moore. And their daughters, Emily, Rachel, Evelyn and Catherine."

Mr. Moore added, "Emily is finishing school in two years. Rachel has three more. Evelyn is in the 6th grade and Cat is in the 4th."

The introductions seemed muted. John was not truly listening. He continued to stare at the eldest girl—he could not help himself. Emily was tall and stood erect. Her eyes were bright and crystal blue. Freckles sprinkled across the bridge of her nose. Her hair—long, copper-colored red streaked with golden highlights—touched the middle of her back. The yellow ribbon holding her cascading curls away from her face matched her pastel dress. John had never seen such beautiful hair or delicate features. She was pure elegance, a gorgeous creature.

John was beginning college in the fall in Dallas. He wondered why she was just now moving to Oak Hill. He was impressed with her politeness. She shook hands with her parents and each of his five brothers. Once he thought she smiled at him but was uncertain. He stepped forward when his name was called. He offered his hand to Mr. Moore, Mrs. Moore and to each of the girls. He was so tongue-tied; he could only tip his head slightly when Emily took his hand. He did not want to let go. Her skin was so soft. He felt everyone's eyes upon him, especially Art's. Embarrassed, he released her hand.

Franklin and Maggie led their guests into the dining room. Art was seated next to Emily who would be in his class at school. Timidly, she listened to Art blabber about school and horses, smiling politely. She often cut her eyes at his older brother. When she'd catch John looking back, she'd look down at her plate or pretend she was listening to Art. She didn't want either boy to notice she was clearly captivated by both.

Art thought she was the prettiest girl in town. He was certain of it. He also thought she looked much older than sixteen. He could imagine all the guys in his class gawking at her the first day of school. Boy, how he could strut around since he'd be the only one who already knew her. He was determined to guard her against all those goons. He continued talking to her during dinner, monopolizing her attention. John sat across the table and between bites of food, watched her every move.

Rachel was seated next to Sam as they, too, were the same age. They talked some but found only a few common interests. Evelyn and Catherine were seated on either side of Willie. But at their ages the opposite sex was most unpleasant, boring, and rumored to carry cooties. Clayton and Paddy, seated at the end of the table, were only glad their parents paid little attention to the number of uneaten vegetables on their plates.

During dinner, Franklin announced that Maggie held a music class on Thursday afternoons. He asked if the girls would be interested in piano lessons. Peg was thrilled and immediately asked Maggie for more details. Peg was certain all four of her girls would want to continue their music lessons. They all could play to some degree. Cat was just learning, but Emily had played for nine years.

Art leaned toward Emily to ask if she played often. She nodded that she did. He told her that he, too, could play. His mom had taught him and his brothers when they were younger. He added that John could play the guitar as well. Eavesdropping, John slumped slightly in his chair when Emily glanced his way.

Emily, looking directly at John, and in a soft, clear voice said, "I would love to take piano lessons, Mrs. Bailey."

Both boys beamed, each thinking now they would see her more often.

Maggie watched the reaction of her two eldest sons. A smile spread across her face. She glanced at Franklin. He was too involved in a conversation with Mr. Moore to notice his sons. The men were discussing the new Model T Runabout coming out in the fall. Franklin added that he had recently ordered the new Kenwood galvanized steel windmill and water tower from the Sears, Roebuck Catalog. Mr. Moore was most interested, wanting to replace the wooden windmill at his place.

Music lessons began promptly the following Thursday. Maggie, pleased the music room was spacious enough for students waiting their turn for lessons, never scheduled more than two at a time. With the Moore girls, she made allowances. Sometimes the girls ventured to the kitchen to see if Tia was baking cookies. Most often, they waited in the gazebo.

Years before, Ernie built the gazebo. He also added an addition to the back of the main house. With its floor-to-ceiling windows, the room was christened the sunroom. Since Franklin had refused rent, Ernie insisted this was his way of thanking them. Maggie, Tia, and Santos planted roses, chrysanthemums, hibiscus, daisies, tulips, hyacinths, and iris around the gazebo. Sometimes in the evenings Franklin and Maggie traded their porch swing conversations for the peacefulness at the gazebo. Together, they walked hand-in-hand down the path to the gazebo and sat on one of the curved benches. The gazebo faced the creek and the view along with the fragrance of the flowers were always inviting.

The gazebo seemed to be the place that Emily Moore chose to wait her turn for piano lessons. Most Thursdays promptly at 4:00 p.m., John came home from working at the drugstore. Before going into the house, he went directly to the gazebo knowing she would be there. Emily always smiled shyly, moving slightly on the bench to make room for him. She rested her leg against his as if the bench were not large enough for them both. She was intrigued by the small patch of dark whiskers growing on his upper lip. Emily glanced at them often as the sun's light cast red streaks through them. She wondered how his kisses tasted and if his whiskers tickled.

Usually, Art arrived about thirty minutes later. John made some excuse he was needed at the house and retreated, leaving them. Art sat on the steps of the gazebo and talked to Emily until Rachel or Evelyn came to get her. Art escorted the girls to the music room and then returned to whatever chore he had left undone.

When the Moore girls started school, Art was true to his promise even though his pledge was unknown to Emily. He sat by her in class and looked for her after school. He wanted one more chance to talk to her before Mr. Moore came and she would have to go home. Soon, Emily became accustomed to his being at her side all the time. She relished his companionship and considered him a good friend. Girls were harder to make friends with it seemed. She even looked forward to the quick peck he'd bestow on her cheek or lips whenever no one was looking.

One Thursday while waiting for her music lessons, she got bored sitting in the gazebo. She walked down to the corral to find Art. He was lunging a horse for its exercise.

"Hey there!" he greeted. "Waiting for your lesson?'

"Hey, yourself, and yes, I am."

"I'm finished here. Come help me brush Chica."

Emily stepped off the corral railing and followed Art as he led the mare into the barn. He tethered Chica in a stall. He used a bristled brush on the horse's under belly and sides. Emily watched a few minutes then asked to try. Art extended the brush. She laughed as she ducked under his arm. She took the brush and made long strokes with it down Chica's sides.

"That feels good, huh, girl?" Art patted the horse's neck.

"So does this," Emily, brush in hand, turned, and grabbed Art's shirt collar. She pulled him closer and kissed him. Not a quick peck. He could feel her heart beating against his. He responded by kissing her again.

"Art," she whispered, as he kissed her neck.

Chica, clearly aggravated being tethered during such folly, stomped her leg. Art quickly stepped away as Evelyn ran into the barn. Emily, embarrassed from getting caught, turned toward her younger sister.

"It's time for your lesson, Emily," Evelyn announced with an impish grin.

Emily straightened her lace collar and tucked some loose curls in place. Before following Evelyn out of the barn, she smiled flirtatiously at Art. Their friendship was now something more.

GOD'S GIFTS

Spring ** Winter 1927

One sunny afternoon following an early spring shower, Maggie was working in the flowerbeds by the gazebo. She was getting the tulip beds ready for new bulbs. Clayton and Paddy were playing with their wooden toys inside the gazebo. Maggie stood, reached for the basket of bulbs sitting on the ground and then collapsed onto the grass. Clayton screamed as he ran toward the barn calling for Santos. Paddy scrambled to the house for Tia. By the time Tia could make any sense of the five-year-old's blubbering, Santos carried Maggie into the kitchen. Clayton followed close behind. Tia urged Santos to take Maggie quickly up the back stairs to her room.

Willie and Art, who had been cleaning horse stalls, had heard Clayton's screams. They rushed from the barn and saw Santos carrying their mother to the house. Willie ran to find John and Sam. Art, without hesitation, pulled Azul away from eating oats in her stall. He swung up on her using her mane as reins and galloped bareback into town for Franklin and Doc Lawrence. When Doc and Franklin arrived, the boys were standing around Maggie's bed. Paddy was snuggled up next to her. She was propped up on bed pillows with a cold rag on her forehead. She smiled meekly as Franklin rushed in. Doc ushered everyone out so he could examine her.

The Bailey family along with Santos and Tia waited in the hallway by the bedroom door. Doc stepped out to tell Franklin

Maggie asked for him. Franklin smiled encouragingly at his sons. He walked into the room and closed the door behind him. Doc was greeted by a group of frightened boys sitting in a huddle on the floor. Tia and Santos, leaning against the wall, looked anxious.

Doc smiled warmly as he said, "Boys, your mom has just been working too hard; that's all. She only fainted—needs bed rest. I know you're worried. I don't think your parents would mind my telling you. You're going to have a little brother or sister by Christmas time."

At first the boys sat silently and then the news began to register across their faces. One by one they stood. Tia watched as the boys' expressions slowly transformed from fright and worry to thankfulness and relief. She saw smiles dancing in their eyes.

Santos rushed to them, grabbing as many as he could at one time. He locked them into a tight bear-hug. He laughed as he embraced them.

"Oh, little Niños, God loves us good, no?" Santos beamed.

John was the first to speak, "I start college this fall. Lucky me! I won't be here for another baby—guess that means you have diaper duty again, Willie."

John was being sarcastic, but Willie was thrilled at the prospect of another baby brother.

One afternoon, Tia tapped softly on Maggie's bedroom door. She edged the door open slowly. Maggie had been asleep but sat up when Tia entered.

"Oh, I'm so sorry to wake you. I came for your lunch tray."

"Delores, please sit down. You've been working so hard. I feel guilty having to stay confined to bed while you take care of the house and my boys."

Tia scooted the tray to one side and sat on the bed. "Just for a few minutes. I have a pot of beans on the stove."

Maggie smiled, "You know, Delores, in the five years you and Santos have lived here, I've never asked why you left South Texas. I don't want to pry. If you'd rather not say, that's fine."

Tia stiffened slightly. Maggie took her hand, "I am prying. I'm sorry."

Tia slowly answered, "No, it's fine." She took a deep breath, "As the years pass, I think or hope I'll forget somehow. To begin Luis and I met in Kingsland. He worked on the Ranch, and I worked in town at the mercantile. We married young and wanted a family more than anything. We each had a slew of siblings. More nieces and nephews than we could count! We had trouble having a baby. For four years we prayed night and day for a baby. Our families felt sorry for us. They blamed me thinking we should have had at least two or three children underfoot. My three sisters pitied me. Years passed. After the eighth year without a baby, we accepted that our family would just be the two of us. Then the tenth year when I was twenty-eight, God blessed us with a son." Tia's voice faltered and her countenance changed. Maggie squeezed her hand, upset with herself for being inquisitive.

"Tomás was all we'd ever dreamed, an answered prayer. He was healthy and spirited and curious, a typical boy. Like yours," she tittered. "Tomás was a beautiful child, dark hair and dark eyes. Luis, of course, could hardly wait for the day he could take his son to the stables and teach him about horses. Tomás was a natural. You'd think he'd been born on a horse's back! When he was twelve, he started competing in local rodeos. Team roping first, then steer wrestling and finally saddle bronc riding. He was good. Won awards, ribbons, and trophies. He loved horses and riding in rodeos. Then when he was sixteen, during a competition, he fell from a bucking horse and broke his neck. He died there in the arena…," Tia paused; tears welled in her eyes. "I didn't get another chance to tell him how much I loved him! I didn't get to tell him goodbye."

Maggie sat helplessly as Tia sobbed deeply. Deep bitter moans surfaced from within the depths of her soul.

"Oh, Delores! I am so sorry!" Maggie scooted closer and enveloped Tia as she would one of her hurting children. She held her tightly until Tia's crying eased.

Tia sat up, "I'm sorry, Maggie. I didn't intend to cry. I never know when it will happen. Sorrow just grips me at times and won't turn loose."

Tia dried her eyes with her hands, "Luis and I tried to stay and continue to live on the Ranch. But it was impossible. Too many memories. So, we packed up and traveled north. We hoped our sad memories would stay behind. But they didn't. They don't, it seems."

"Oh, Delores, I should have never asked." Maggie's tears tumbled down her cheeks.

"No, no, Maggie, I should have told you long before. Luis and I love it here. We have secretly adopted your niños as our own."

Maggie smiled, "And they have adopted you."

Tia hugged Maggie tightly then picked up the tray. "Get some rest, dear one."

Lucinda Mae and Loraine Rae were born two days before Christmas, December 23, 1927. Not one gift, but two incredibly special gifts bestowed to the Bailey household of boys. They were fraternal twins. Lucinda had a full head of dark hair. Loraine was practically bald. Both were beautiful and perfect in every way. As the family sat in the study by the heat of the fireplace that Christmas Eve, Maggie placed the girls on the ottoman. She opened out their crocheted baby blankets, Lucinda's white, Loraine's yellow. She wanted the boys to see their baby sisters dressed in matching white lace gowns trimmed with pink ribbons. A white drawstring tied the ends of their gowns around their feet, concealing their tiny pink socks.

John was home from college on Christmas break when the girls were born. Surprisingly enough, he was not anxious to return. All the boys, even Santos, waited their turn to hold these wee novelties. Franklin was so proud of his little girls.

Franklin kissed Maggie's hands. "Oh, Maggie girl, look at our family! This is the best Christmas present I've ever had!"

Sitting on the oval rug in front of the hearth, Willie watched his older brothers with his baby sisters. Cleary disappointed, he had wanted another brother. Hearing his father's declaration, he exclaimed fearfully, "Are they all we get for Christmas?"

Everyone laughed at him. Willie ducked his head in shame.

"Willie, come here," Maggie motioned for her nine-year-old. She wrapped her arms around him and whispered, "You may choose one gift under the tree to open now if you'd like."

Willie hurried to the Christmas tree which sat in the corner of the room. He dropped on his knees to study the size of the packages that bore his name. Clay and Paddy looked eagerly toward their mother. Maggie nodded at them. All three boys crowded in front of the tree trimmed in silver garland, red ribbons and pinecones. They arranged their packages on the floor to determine which one most worthy of opening.

Franklin lit his pipe and smiled at his wife as his younger sons ripped into their chosen gifts. "This is indeed a wonderful Christmas!"

SUMMER AWAY

Summer 1928

Summer arrived on schedule. Hot, blustery days and humid nights. Heralding the end of another school semester and the beginning of carefree days, at least for the younger children. John remained in Dallas taking a few more finance courses to fulfill his college graduation requirements. Art busied himself doing what he loved most, caring for and training horses. Paying close attention, Art soaked up all Santos taught him. Sam assisted Franklin with the inventory at the drugstore. William, Clay, and Paddy helped with whatever small chores Maggie assigned. Mostly they spent their day playing in the tree house, shooting marbles, skimming stones, or swimming at the creek.

One mid-morning in June, Peg Moore and her girls arrived at the Baileys for one last music lesson before summer break. Maggie greeted them at the door and led them to the music room.

"Thank you, for this, Maggie," Peg said. "I know it's an inconvenient time for you. George has a meeting in town and will be back in a couple of hours to pick us up."

"Nonsense, I'm always happy to see you. My, don't you all look smart."

"We're catching the 1:00 p.m. train for Dallas to visit my brother and his family. A family reunion of sorts. I've not seen my eldest niece since she married, and she recently had a baby. My nephew is coming home from college for the summer. We're staying a week, but Emily is remaining through August. She and my youngest niece, Patrice, are the same ages. Now, where are those adorable baby girls?"

The Moore girls filed into the music room. Evelyn and Cat rushed to the playpen to fuss over Lucy and Loraine. The twins, now six-months-old, were surrounded by teddy bears and cloth baby dolls. Rachel sat on the piano bench and began practicing scales. The younger Moore girls took turns holding Lucy. Peg lifted up Loraine and carried her to the Queen Anne chair. Peg sat down and placed the baby on her knee.

As Peg held Loraine's hands, she sang, "The King of France with twenty thousand men, went up the hill, and then came down again." Peg stretched out her legs causing Loraine to lean backwards against her knees. Loraine squealed with glee.

"Emily, you look nice," Maggie complemented Emily. Emily's dress was pale blue organza with a rounded neck and puffed sleeves above her elbow. White pearl buttons were evenly spaced down the front of the bodice. Pleats, beginning at the waistline, softly fell eight inches above one-strapped black dress shoes.

"Thank you, Mrs. Bailey," Emily twirled her white straw hat uneasily.

"Would you mind asking Tia to bring tea?"

"Of course," Emily placed her hat on the top of the piano, grateful to be released and dashed to the kitchen. She pushed open the door. Tia was washing garden vegetables in a small, galvanized tub in the sink.

Tia greeted her warmly, "Well, hello, Emily."

"Hello, Tia. Mrs. Bailey asked if you'd bring tea to the music room. Is Art at the barn?"

"Yes, where else?" Tia laughed. "He and Santos have plans to go to town for supplies later this afternoon. For now, he's there."

Emily waved her thanks. She hurried out the door, past the gazebo, and down the path to the barn. The double doors were wide open. The horses had been let out earlier that morning to graze in the pasture. The barn was quiet. Art was sitting on a stool in front of a wooden saddle rack cleaning a saddle. A calico barn cat, tail curled around her, lay sleeping on a pile of hay in the first horse stall. Art stood as Emily walked closer.

"Emily, what are you doing here?"

"Are there hourly visitation restrictions, Mr. Bailey?"

"No!" he grinned and wiped the saddle soap from his hands with a towel. "Just surprised, pleasantly surprised! Wow! You look wonderful."

"How wonderful?"

Art leaned toward her and kissed her cheek.

"What was that?"

"Your nice dress and all. I must smell like a horse!"

Emily pulled him closer and kissed him. "Oh, Art, I'm leaving for Dallas for the summer. I'll miss you so much!"

"Wait, what?"

"My mom made arrangements with my aunt and uncle. I'm spending the summer again with my cousin Patrice. My uncle wants to show me the Medical School in Dallas. If I decide to study there, you'll come with me, right? Art, just think how wonderful that would be. We can see each other all the time! No sneaking off to the creek or climbing up in the hayloft!"

"Em, we've talked about this." Art took her hand and led her to the gazebo. They sat on the bench facing the creek. "I don't want to go to college. Well not after graduation anyway. I want to be a rancher and raise horses."

"Oh, Art! How can you make any kind of money doing that?"

"Emily, ranching is a good business. We've talked about this."

"I thought you loved me!"

Art put his arm around her shoulders and pulled her close.

"You know I do," he whispered. "We'll be graduating in May. There's plenty of time to think about our future. Don't worry about that now."

"But I do," Emily looked up, frustrated.

Her crystal blue eyes pierced him through and through. Art was mesmerized by her beauty. His beauty. He kissed her. Fearful of wrinkling her dress, he stood and pulled her to her feet. He stroked her cheek and brushed his fingers softly across her lips.

"Em, you are my future. Don't you know that? The doctor and the rancher. Can't you see us?"

She stomped one foot, clearly pouting, "I don't want to go! I don't want to spend my summer away from you! You'll probably ask Marilee Lawrence or that Janie Calloway girl to swim with you in the creek. Or spread a blanket out on the hill to watch the stars."

"Em, Em, you know you're the only girl for me," he pulled her close and kissed her neck. He deeply breathed in her perfume as if this moment would carry him throughout the summer. "Em, write to me? I want to hear about everything you're doing. I'll count the days 'til your return. We can plan our future then, okay?"

She hugged him tightly, feeling his arm muscles surround her as they embraced. He tilted her chin and kissed her once more.

THE BIG DAY

Spring 1929

The year passed quickly. Another high school graduation arrived. This time for Art and Emily and Marilee Lawrence, Doc Lawrence's daughter. A barbecue was planned for the entire graduating class and their families. The Moores, the Bonds, the Lawrences, and the Baileys, per Franklin's insistence, were hosting the party at the Bailey's.

Tia and Santos were busy helping with all the preparations. Maggie, Peg, and Elizabeth had indeed planned a big day. Franklin's mother, Bessie, was coming by train from Oklahoma in a few days. Gram and Pops, Maggie's parents, had already arrived and were staying with Ernie and Elizabeth. Maggie and Ernie were surprised their father took time away from his farm. They dared not ask too many questions. Pops might decide Mr. Haney, who had been his right-hand man for decades, wouldn't be able to manage without him.

Lucy and Loraine demanded so much of her time, but Maggie still gave piano lessons on Thursdays. The younger Moore girls, Elizabeth's two girls and one other girl from town were her students. Even with the barbecue coming up, she would not say she was too busy. Rachel lost interest when the required one hour of daily practice took her away from her friends. Emily, finding music lessons frivolous, stopped lessons her senior year. She wanted to excel in her studies and gain a scholarship to medical college.

One afternoon a week before graduation, Rachel accompanied Evelyn and Cat to their piano lessons. She peeked into the library and wandered down to the sunroom glancing around as if looking for someone. She pushed open the kitchen door and found Tia busy at the counter peeling potatoes for dinner.

"Come in, Rachel. How nice to see you."

Tia watched as Rachel leaned over a bowl of purple grapes on the counter. How much she had changed over the last couple of years. Being fifteen, she was no longer a little girl. She had blossomed into a pretty, young woman. Her hair was dark, but just as curly as her older sister's. Her eyes were light brown—the color of cocoa. Emily's and Rachel's features and mannerisms were as different as night and day. Rachel had a pleasing manner and a wonderful laugh. Tia always enjoyed her company.

"Tia, do you know where Art is this afternoon?" Rachel asked as she picked a couple of grapes and plopped them into her mouth.

"Yes, sweetheart, he is helping Santos at the barn. We have a new filly. Have you seen her? Go see---" Tia had not stopped peeling potatoes but merely smiled as Rachel kissed her cheek.

"Thanks for the grapes!" Rachel called as she hurried out the back door.

Rachel walked into the barn. The smell of sweet oats and hay filled her nostrils. She loved coming here. Art had taught her to ride—well, he had taught her only because she tagged along with Emily.

When she thought about it, she always seemed to be with Art and Emily. A social club of sorts—Emily and Art, Sam and Trina Jones, James Crowder and Marilee Lawrence, and she and Billy Jeter. The four couples enjoyed fishing at the creek, horseback riding, singing around the piano, or sitting and talking on the porch. They attended the county fair 4-H shows, family barbecues and church picnics. And of course, baseball games at the high school—they did everything together. Even though she and Billy and Sam and Trina were younger—only by two years—they were never excluded.

Art was standing at the far end of the barn brushing down a gelding. The light was too dim for Rachel to tell which horse was being brushed, Samson or Joe. They were both bays. She remembered the first time she called them brown. Art quickly corrected her. Reddish-brown colored horses with black tails and manes were bays; white horses were greys. Rachel stepped softly with intentions to startle him, but Art said hello before she was three feet away.

"How do you do that?" she asked jokingly.

"Joe's ears perked up. He warns me against nosy girls all the time. What are you doin' out here? Is Emily with you?" He resumed brushing the horse's sides and tail as he glanced toward the barn door.

"No, but I've come to see the filly. Tia told me. Where is she?"

"I'm almost finished here, then I'll show you."

Rachel watched as Art cleaned Ole Joe's hooves. Resting his back against Joe's side, Art bent down and pinched the horse's fetlock. Lifting the horse's back left leg, Art balanced it between his knees. Using a hoof pick, he cleaned out dried mud and grass from around the rim of the hoof.

Rachel leaned against a stall railing as Art worked. Azul poked her head over the railing and nickered at her. Rachel placed her hands on both sides of the mare's head. She rubbed her hands over Azul's eyes and down her neck. She placed her cheek against the horse's nose.

"I love to feel a horse's nose, don't you? What does Azul mean anyway?"

"It's "blue" in Spanish. Her coat is so black it looks midnight blue. Pretty, isn't she? She's Santos's mare—brought her here from South Texas. Don't know how old she is really. She's a great horse. Aren't you, girl?"

Art flipped the grooming brush and hoof pick into a tackle box and joined Rachel. He stroked Azul's head. "How 'bout the filly? Ready to see her?"

Rachel followed Art to the other end of the barn. Baby, a palomino mare, was standing toward the back of the stall eating oats from a feed trough. The filly was lying on hay strewn over the ground in the stall. When the filly saw them at the gate, she stood on her long thin legs and stepped toward them.

"Oh, Art! She is beautiful. What's her name?" Rachel leaned over the railing to smooth the white fluff of hair on the filly's head.

"Not sure, yet. Papa said we could name her. We just can't all agree. Willie likes Sugar. Clayton chose Pumpkin and Paddy wants to call her Jingle. Sam doesn't care. Everyone has their favorite. With five of us deciding, she may never have a name. Hey, there, Baby. What a good mama you are."

The mare turned from her feed trough and walked up to the rail where Rachel and Art stood. Baby pushed her head into Rachel's shoulder a couple of times. A gentle reminder she, too, liked to be petted and loved on.

"Art, I need to talk to you. Do you have a minute?" Rachel turned from the horses, looking serious, all kidding aside.

"What a look! What? Need help with math again? Having trouble with Billy Jeter? Is he treating you right? He better be! He's coming with you to the barbecue, right?" Art quickly spurted out questions before Rachel could reply.

"Oh, it's nothing like that. Billy and I are fine. Art, can we go to the creek? I really need to talk to you. I would rather it not be in here, okay?" She turned to exit the barn, hoping he would follow.

"Hey! Wait up! What's so important Baby can't hear?" He laughed at his own joke. He followed Rachel until she was at the edge of the creek, seated under an old oak tree.

"Okay, lady of mystery, what do you want to tell me?" He plopped down next to her and pulled up a long piece of grass to chew on.

"I don't know where to start. You of all people need to know. I found out only yesterday," she hesitated.

He raised his eyebrows, motioning her to continue. "Art," she began again, "I…this is so hard...well, there is no easy way to say it. So here it is. Emily and John are engaged!"

Art bounded up from the ground in one swift movement. "What? What are you talking about?" He grabbed Rachel up from the ground and held her arms tightly, slightly shaking her. She'd never lied before, but this could not possibly be true.

"Emily and John have been writing to each other since last summer. Art, I never knew! She said all those letters she received were from a good friend. She never said anything about John, well, not that much anyway. I thought all the letters she received were from her friend, Betty. John proposed in his last letter, and she accepted! They are going to make the announcement when he comes home for the barbecue. My mom and dad know now—Emily told them yesterday, but I don't think yours know. I'm so sorry, Art. I know how you feel about Emily. I know how hurt you'd be! And *you* most of all, should know. I hope you don't hate me for telling you. I…"

He placed his hand gently across her lips.

"Stop, Rachel. Please, please, don't say another word. You're making this up, right? It's a joke—a terrible joke?" He looked into her teary eyes but could tell she was telling the truth.

Art stepped a few steps backwards. He intently searched her eyes hoping he had misunderstood. He placed his hands on either side his head, turned, and walked toward the creek. As he neared the water's edge, he bent over double as if kicked in the gut by a horse. Rachel watched him helplessly, her eyes welling with tears. Oh, how she hated her sister at this moment.

He mumbled something she did not understand. He turned toward her. As he walked past, he said, "Rae, I don't hate you. Not you. Never will. You know your way back to the house."

He slowly walked back to the barn, leaving her sobbing under the big oak tree.

When Franklin came home that evening, he hung his hat on the rack in the mudroom and opened the door into the kitchen. The smell of roasted chicken and stewed tomatoes baking in the oven encased the room. Tia and Elizabeth were huddled at the kitchen table whispering over cups of hot coffee. As Frank entered, Tia stood to greet him and offered him a cup of coffee.

"Thanks, but I'll wait for dinner. Hey, are you two scheming about the barbecue without Maggie? Where is she—with the girls?"

"Lucy and Loraine are both asleep, Franklin. Maggie is in the library," Elizabeth answered.

Franklin squeezed her shoulder and went to search for his wife. Maggie was leaning against a pillow on one end of the royal blue love seat; her legs curled under her. Her left elbow was resting on the armrest and her right hand was covering her eyes.

"Hello, beautiful," Franklin announced softly as he entered the room. "Are you hiding from the children?"

He kissed Maggie as she looked up. As she stretched her legs to the floor, she held out a letter that had been lying across her lap.

"What's this?"

She looked so upset he immediately began to read. "It's from John. He will be able to come to the barbecue after all! That's great! Why would that upset you, hon?"

"Read on," Maggie instructed.

Franklin sat down beside his wife. Out of habit he began to read aloud. "Cla*sses end this week for the summer. I have taken some extra time off work. Mr. Stiles will hold my job at the bank until August. And here's the most wonderful news. I have asked Emily to marry me, and she has accepted*! What? When did this happen? John's only home for a few days for Christmas and one week during the summer. He goes to school and works twelve hours a week at the bank. How did this happen?"

He waved the letter around, looking at Maggie for answers. She shook her head. Looking through teary eyes, she motioned him to continue. "*I am coming home a few days early to see Mr. Moore and formally ask for Emily's hand. I know he will agree. I've thought this through. I've saved enough money to pay for a JP and used my last two months' salary to buy an engagement ring. I'll give it to her as a graduation present. We plan a small July 4th wedding—just family. Then I'll leave, as usual, the 1st of September to finish my last semester. We'll need a place to stay until then. We can either stay with* *her parents or with you if that's not too much to ask. When I return to Dallas in September, I'll find a more suitable place to live. Then send for Emily. If she comes to school here, then we'll find something together. Anyway, Dallas has a wonderful medical school...* What? A wedding next month? Has Peg said anything to you?"

"No, this is the first I've heard," placing her hand on his arm. "Franklin, my heart is so troubled, so torn. One half is joyous for John, if Emily is indeed God's life-mate for him. But can he finish school and provide for her? What if his career takes him elsewhere while she's still in school? What about her plans—her scholarship in Galveston? How can they both manage being in school at the same time? Will George pay for Emily's schooling if she goes to Dallas or expect that of John? Starting out can be so difficult. You and I can attest to that! They're so young, like we were! Why did he not tell us how he felt until now?"

"And poor Art, my heart is splitting in two for him. He will be devastated! You know how he dotes on Emily. He adores her. I think his intention is marriage as well. I just don't understand. Emily will be a wonderful daughter-in-law, that's true. Oh, Franklin, what are we to do? Our sons are in love with the same girl!"

Franklin put his arms around Maggie as she cried into his shoulder. His mind was spinning as he digested the news. He had certainly not seen this coming! Why had Emily not said anything? Why had John not talked to him about his plans? He needed to talk to George, and of course, John when he arrived. But now his priority was Art.

"Maggie, sweetheart, come have coffee with the ladies. You need their company right now. I'm going out to find Art, okay?" He took her hand and escorted her to the kitchen.

"Tia, dinner may be a delayed this evening." He kissed Maggie's cheek as she sat down at the table. He glanced back as Elizabeth squeezed Maggie's hand.

Franklin found Art at their favorite fishing spot at the creek. He consoled his son for hours. They agreed Art would stay with Uncle Ernie to sort things out. Art did not want to be around when John came home—not now, he needed time to think. When Art asked if he should talk to Emily, Franklin advised that decision was solely his to make. Oh, this is all so troublesome!

The next morning's silence around the breakfast table was as thick as Santos's day-old coffee. Franklin had explained to the children at dinner the evening before that Art was visiting Gram and Pops at Uncle Ernie's. He felt no other explanation was needed.

Maggie was so worried. She had not seen Art since John's letter had arrived. She busied about doing household chores and caring for Lucy and Loraine. She could think of nothing else no matter how hard she tried. Peg came mid-afternoon the next day to visit. The women sat together on the sofa in the parlor. Both were totally perplexed and bewildered. Peg tried explaining Emily's feelings as revealed to her only the night before. Maggie listened but thought them trivial and inexcusable. Peg and Maggie hugged each other and vowed to pray for their children.

Three days later, Maggie and Tia were doing the dishes after dinner—Tia washed, Maggie dried. Maggie placed a dried plate on the counter as Willie bounded through the kitchen door.

"Joe's in his stall! Art's home!"

Maggie thanked him as Willie ran past to share the good news with the rest of the family. She placed her dishtowel on the counter.

Tia looked up from the sudsy wash pan and swooshed her hand, "Maggie, Go! Just go! I'll finish here!"

Maggie gently squeezed Tia's arm as she turned toward the door. "Thank you."

Maggie opened the door and stepped into the night's mantle of darkness. Peaches, curled at the bottom of the step, rose and eagerly followed. Stopping to look up at the start-lit sky, Maggie prayed silently. She continued to the gazebo. Art was not there.

She walked toward the stone house. Santos, sitting on the porch, sharpened knives on a whetstone straddled across his knees. An old coal-oil lantern, his only light, sat beside him. Santos looked up when he heard footsteps. He nodded his head toward the horse barn.

"He's there, Señora."

Nodding her thanks, Maggie and Peaches strolled across the yard to the barn. The barn door was slightly opened. Peaches squeezed through. Maggie followed into the quiet, dark barn. As she passed each stall, she peered inside. One by one—Samson, Joe, Pico, Chica, Azul, Banjo, Duke, and Baby—all accounted for except Art and the filly. As she approached the last stall used to store extra hay, Peaches ran past her. Maggie squinted into the dark shadows. There on the floor leaning against a bale of hay sat Art. Peaches lay beside him on one side: the filly on the other. Art's hat pulled down low over his eyes concealed his face; his elbows rested on his drawn-up knees.

"Mama," he said softly, chewing on a long piece of hay.

Maggie entered the stall, shooed Peaches to one side and sat down. The two sat in silence for what seemed an eternity to Maggie. Finally, Art spoke.

"Saw her today. She looked nervous, beautiful as always, but nervous—you know how she fiddles her fingers when she's nervous? Well, Emily seemed shocked I was upset! Got all defensive. She thought we were just friends—that's all—*just friends*. Said she's loved John ever since the first time she saw him. Certainly, wasn't obvious to me! If she loved John as much as she claims, why was she always around me? At school, at church, here? Why would she hold my hand or go with me on long walks? Or let me hold her close when we danced? Or let me kiss her or plan our future together if she loved him? Answer that! She said she didn't mean to hurt me. She thought I'd be happy for her! Happy for *her*? Can you believe that?" Maggie choked down her emotions and remained composed. Art continued to vent.

"All this year she's been writing letters to John! Remember her talking about her friend Betty Garrett? Well, Betty's brother, Simon, is going to the same college as John—what a coincidence, right? Simon and John became friends. Emily's cousin Patrice was best friends with you guessed it, Betty! It seems the past two summers when Emily was supposedly visiting Patrice, guess who else showed up? That's right! Good ole brother John—he told *us* he was working and couldn't come home—working! I bet! What a lie! He was messing with my girl! They're both liars!" He took off his hat and angrily tossed it across the stall. The filly, spooked by the sudden movement, began to fidget and nicker. Peaches, too, sat up suddenly and looked around. The filly, quickly calmed by Art's whispers, settled back on the straw. Art rubbed the dog's head and she curled back down.

"Mama, I've been thinking. I wanted to leave today, but Papa asked me to stay for you—for graduation and the barbecue. I'll do that. I appreciate the party you're giving me. I really do, but I can't stay and watch them together. The idea of them getting married sickens me!" Maggie took his hand as he leaned against her shoulder. "I'll stay with Uncle Ernie to be out of the way—John's way. I have been thinking about getting a job down in the Valley on the King Ranch!"

He sat up and looked into her eyes as she clung to his hand. "You know how much I love horses. Aw, I know what you're thinking. What about college? I'll go later or I'll find one down there. I don't care about college, really. Santos offered to introduce me to his family who work on the Ranch. I can make a good living there."

He leaned back against her shoulder. "You know, I would have followed Emily anywhere. I just want to be with her! I thought I knew her. Now, I don't know where she's going or what's she's thinking! She would often ask if I loved her. But would always change the subject when I answered yes. She belittled my love for ranching—now I know why! Mama, does John really know her?

Does he know she's always wanted to be a doctor? That she earned a scholarship to Galveston? Does he know that when she pouts, she stomps her foot? Does he know that her favorite color is pink? But she's afraid to wear it thinking the color clashes with her hair. Does he know when she is angry, she bites her bottom lip? Or when she's nervous, she fiddles with her fingers as if playing the piano? Has he smelled her hair scented with lavender and hibiscus?

Has he watched her twirl her hair around her finger when she reads? Has he heard how high she squeals when she jumps into the creek? Has he seen her little devious smile when she's teasing? Does he know that when she rides bareback, she tucks her hair up into her hat? She rides full out until her hat flips off and her copper hair flows free. That glorious hair! And how many times has he drowned in those beautiful, blue eyes? Mama, he can't possibly love her more than I do!"

"Oh, Arthur," Maggie managed to say.

Art slipped down to rest his head in her lap. She rubbed his shoulders and back. She combed his hair away from his forehead with her fingers. Tears streamed down her face as she remembered how he liked to lie across her lap to have his back rubbed when he was a little boy.

They remained silent for several minutes. With a trembling voice, Maggie said, "Art, honey, I can't stand seeing you hurt so. It breaks my heart seeing you like this. You don't have to stay for the graduation ceremony or for the barbecue, for that matter, just to please me. Your father and I just want you to be happy. Baby, there's a girl out there who will win your heart. Believe me, she is waiting for you. And she'll be very blessed to be loved by you."

He hugged her legs. He sat up and kissed her cheek. He smacked his lips, "Umm, kinda salty."

They laughed and held hands as they leaned against the bale of hay. They listened to the horses' whinnies, the croaking frogs, and the chirping crickets. Art kissed his mother's cheek again, insisting it was late. She should get some rest before the big day. He helped her up and held her hand as he escorted her out of barn. At the gazebo, Maggie hugged him tightly, not wanting to let him go. She kissed his cheeks and his lips before turning away. Peaches led her back to the house. When she neared the porch, Maggie looked back over her shoulder. Art, still standing on the path, waved and turned toward the barn.

CONFRONTATIONS AND CONFESSIONS

Spring 1929

Mid-morning the next day, Sam came through the front door and stood in the foyer to announce John's arrival. Paddy and Clayton rushed from the kitchen and pounced on John's back. John feeling outnumbered quickly dropped his bag on the floor. Paddy hung onto John's neck as Clayton grasped John's shoulder. John spun the boys around. Not wanting to fall off, the boys clinched their holds tightly. When the spin ended, the boys scooted off John's back. Taking full advantage of double-teaming, they grabbed John's legs. John slightly pushed them away, holding them at arm's length.

Tia, hearing the commotion from the kitchen, hurried down the hall to welcome John home. She smiled broadly as John enveloped her into a big bear-hug-squeeze. Franklin opened the doors to the study. At the sight of their father, the boys stood at attention as if they were soldiers and a general had entered the room. John turned and extended his hand for a handshake.

Franklin took John's hand and pulled him into a hug. "Welcome home, son."

Glancing over his father's shoulder, John saw his mother approaching from the study. With tears in her eyes, Maggie hugged John tightly. Franklin suggested Paddy and Clayton help Tia in the kitchen. He and Maggie wanted to talk to John before the guests arrived.

Placing an arm around each shoulder, Tia herded the younger boys to the kitchen. As the boys begrudgingly passed by, Sam grinned.

"We still have melons to slice. You can't get out of work just because John is home!" Tia teased as she pushed open the kitchen door.

Looking thoughtfully at his parents, John mentioned the Moores would be here soon. They were only ten minutes or so behind him. Franklin patted John's shoulder gently. Turning toward the study, Franklin said, "I think we have a lot to talk about, don't you?"

John and Maggie followed Franklin into the study. Franklin closed the double doors behind them.

Sam went outside and stood on the front porch waiting for the Moores. He was really waiting for Rachel. He had been worried about her the last couple of days. With all the talk of John and Emily and their wedding, Rachel had been visibly upset.

The Moore's Model-T pulled up the driveway. Sam stepped down the porch steps and briskly walked toward the car. George Moore got out and came around the front of the car to open the passenger door for Peg.

"Mr. Moore, Mrs. Moore," Sam greeted as the girls filed out from the backseat.

As Cat and Evelyn walked toward the porch, Sam told them they'd find the kids in the kitchen with Tia. The two girls hurried up the steps hoping Tia had baked their favorite cinnamon-sugar cookies.

Emily stepped onto the side runner. Sam offered his hand for assistance. She thanked him and followed her parents to the house. Her red hair, twisted into a roll, was secured at the nape of her neck. She had refused to cut it as was the fashion just to be part of a silly trend. She wore a dark blue tight-fitting jacket opened over a light blue chiffon skirt. Her lacy white chemise worn under a white silk blouse completed her outfit.

Rachel, however, had cut her hair. Its thick waves touched the bottom of her ear lobes. Sam preferred her hair long and free flowing, but he certainly had no say in the matter. She did have a pretty neck though, he thought. Rachel stepped from the car. He extended his hand, but she nervously grabbed his arm. Her bright yellow organza shift did little to boost any brightness to her mood.

"What's going on, Sam? Where's Art?" Rachel whispered. Sam leaned closer and briefly explained the latest events as they entered the house.

Tia met the Moores at the door. She invited George, Peg, and Emily to join Gram and Pops in the sunroom. Lemonade and cookies were being served there. The children were in the kitchen with Elizabeth. Tia reminded Sam that he was to help Ernie and Santos and Jim Carson set up tables and park cars. The Jeters and the Lawrences would be arriving soon.

"Yes, Ma'am," he answered, but remained in the foyer until the adults were out of sight.

When she was certain she had not been seen, Rachel stepped from the parlor and joined Sam in the foyer. They moved toward the oak bench in the alcove under the stairwell. It was conveniently situated facing the study. They sat down. Sam could see Rachel was upset. He truly felt sorry for her. She was taking this badly. Sam sat a few minutes longer then apologized, telling Rachel he was needed outside. Rachel smiled weakly. He patted her hand as he stood to leave.

Rachel sat quietly listening to the voices coming from the study. She recognized each voice but could not understand what was being said. She looked down at her hands. She wondered how long she had clenched them so tightly. The palms of her hands were sweaty; her fingernails indented the flesh. She smoothed the wrinkles from her dress and checked the buckles on her low-heeled tan pumps. She thought she heard a noise on the stairs above her and looked up.

Willie and Tip sat on the very top step. Willie waved; she waved back.

She was surprised when Emily plopped down on the bench beside her. Emily did not say a word, but she, too, stared at the doors to the study. Rachel moved over not wanting any part of her body touching her sister's. The girls had barely spoken. When they did, an argument was initiated by one or the other, never ending well.

After a few more minutes of anxiety and agony, the doors of the study opened. Rachel and Emily stood to their feet. Franklin and Maggie walked from the room. Franklin had his arm around Maggie. She had been crying. Emily wanted to rush to her to explain so many things. Since she did not know exactly what to say or where to start, she remained still.

Franklin smiled, "Good morning, Rachel. Let's join the others, shall we? I could use some lemonade, couldn't you?"

He held out his arm and she had no choice but to take it. She looked over her shoulder as John walked toward Emily. He took her hand and led her to the study. Once more the doors closed.

Willie scooted slowly down the stair steps but remained on the landing. He pressed his face against the gaps in the railing. Tip darted down the first flight of steps before Willie could grab him. The dog stopped at the closed doors. Wagging his tail, Tip sniffed underneath it. The dog looked back at his ten-year-old master as if to say, "You can hear better down here!" Willie smiled as he tip-toed across the wood floor to the study.

When he eased down against the wall, Willie noticed that one of the study doors was not completely closed. He rubbed Tip's head and whispered, "Good boy!"

Willie pressed his body against the closed door and listened. If he turned his head just a certain way, he could see through the crack between the doors. John and Emily sat facing each other in the wing-back chairs near the fireplace. He heard John's soft, low voice.

"Emily, you know how much I love you. I was terribly wrong to jump ahead like this and think only about my studies. We can wait to marry, can't we? A few months won't be that long. Why did you not tell me about your scholarship? That's wonderful! Emily, you must go to school in Galveston, and I'll go to Dallas. You cannot let this opportunity go! We…"

Emily interrupted him, her voice almost panicked, "But I want to get married! I want to marry you, John, now—right now. I want to leave here and be with you wherever you are."

John stood. He paced the floor in front of the fireplace as if rehearsing how to respond. He looked at her thoughtfully and lovingly. He sat back in the chair facing her and placed his hands over hers.

"Emily, are you afraid I won't wait for you?" He asked, searching her eyes. Emily turned her head slightly, hiding her distorted face. John knelt in front of her chair and pulled her close. She leaned into his embrace.

"Emmy, I'll never leave you." With his fingertips, he brushed away a tear escaping down her nose. "I would be foolish to do that! My parents and your parents are right, you know. We should wait at least until I finish school. I can go to summer school and finish earlier. You should go to Galveston and begin…"

Emily began to sob, lowering her head onto John's shoulder. "Emmy, it's the only practical way. Don't you see? When I finish school, we'll be married. I'll come to Galveston and find a position there. We'll live there until you finish school. You must promise me you'll go!"

He lifted her left hand and slowly twisted her engagement ring from her finger.

She gasped, "No, John! Don't do this!"

"Emmy, please wear this ring as my pledge to marry you in September." He placed the gold ring back on her finger. "It's not much and someday I'll get you a better ring. A bigger diamond, one you deserve. I promise you'll have only the very best. But with this ring, we are pledged to each other now and forever."

Emily stopped crying as he lifted her left hand. He kissed the simple gold band with the tiny diamond in its center. As he wiped the tears from her cheeks with the back of his fingertips, she smiled at him.

"Emmy, I have to ask one thing." She looked at him anxiously. "Was there or is there anything between you and Art? Is that why you want to leave now?"

Emily stood abruptly. She walked to the fireplace and faced the mantle. With one finger, she slowly traced the imprint of an almond blossom carved in the white marble. She lowered her head and twisted the engagement ring on her finger. Without turning around, she said, "We were friends, school chums. We went everywhere together. He was my best friend in school. I told you that in my letters. At least, I thought we were just friends—I thought he felt the same."

Taking a deep breath, she continued. "We wanted different things after graduation, different lives. I've always known I'd be a doctor. He wanted to be a rancher, of all ridiculous things. What kind of future is that? Anyway, we had fun in school—that's all—he's fun to be around. He was always a gentleman and when I was with him…" She suddenly hushed before saying too much and revealing true feelings.

John moved up behind her and placed his arms around her waist and leaned his head against the back of hers. "I know—I know, but I think we have both hurt him deeply."

Emily's body became rigid. "I love only you," she whispered between sobs. She turned suddenly and put her arms around his neck, pulling him closer.

"Only you, John, only you," she repeated as she lifted her head from his shoulder.

He wiped the tears from her cheeks and obligingly kissed her softly.

Willie wrinkled his nose and scrambled to his feet as the front bell rang. He heard voices coming down the hallway from the sunroom. Tip bounced on all fours as he barked at the doorbell. Willie snapped his fingers at the dog, trying to distract him. The dog would not be silenced. Willie turned and ran down the hall through the archway into the dining room. As he burst through the adjoining door to the kitchen, he bumped into Aunt Elizabeth.

"Sorry!" he apologized. He raced through the kitchen and grabbed a couple of cookies cooling on a rack as he passed. Without breaking stride, he ran through the mudroom and hit the back door. Tip, always enjoying a good chase, raced behind.

The barbecue was a great success. Almost every family representing the graduating honorees was in attendance. Wonderful dishes covered the picnic tables—fried chicken, barbecue beef, potato salad, hard-boiled eggs, baked beans, fresh fruit and steamed vegetables. The dessert table held several varieties of cookies and pies, and Aunt Elizabeth's famous chocolate cake.

Jim Carson and several other men brought their stringed instruments. One by one, they removed their guitars or fiddles or banjos from their cases. They tuned up in the gazebo. The younger folks and some of the older couples, too, grabbed partners. Soon a dance was underway. The boys, who had no interest in girls or dancing, started a baseball game in the pasture. The younger girls took turns swinging from the four rope swings which hung from the elm trees in the front yard. Other children played chase dodging around the women who were sitting on quilts spread on the ground. The men stood in groups eating and talking. Everyone was having a good time, or so it seemed.

Maggie had not seen Art all afternoon. She didn't really expect to see him since he hadn't attended his graduation ceremony. Ernie assured her that he had come to the barbecue. Being a good hostess, Maggie made her way around the yard greeting guests.

Franklin spotted her. Slipping his arm around her, he led her toward the gazebo. With the guitars playing softly, they began to dance. Maggie felt comfort in her husband's arms. As the next tune began, Art tapped his dad on the shoulder.

"May I cut in?" After hugging his son, Franklin stood aside.

Art took his mother's right hand and rested his right hand at the small of her back. The instruments continued to play. "Mama, I'm leaving now."

Maggie started to object, but Art squeezed her hand. "You know I'll be fine. I've told the family goodbye. John found me earlier today. We talked—he explained some things and tried to convince me to stay. I have not changed my mind. I cannot stay, Mama. I'm going to Kingsville. Santos sent a telegram ahead of me. The train leaves in an hour."

Maggie's eyes welled with tears as she whispered, "Art, oh, Art."

Smiling bravely, she desperately tried to think of something to say to her son who was hurting so deeply. If she could only impart some bit of wisdom or perhaps say a prayer of encouragement to carry with him as he departed into the world on his own. On his own…she suddenly realized he was leaving home like a baby bird pushed from its nest.

After taking a deep breath, she could only whisper, "I love you, Art."

"I know, Mama."

Maggie laid her head against her son's shoulder as they finished their dance. She softly squeezed his hand. Her little boy had become a man.

NEW BEGINNINGS

FALL 1929

When the first of August arrived, John accompanied the Moores to the train station to see Emily off to Galveston. She enrolled at the Texas Medical School. After his graduation from Business College in Dallas, John and Emily were married in a private ceremony at the Bailey's on September 2, 1929. Maggie and Peg were both insistent their children's wedding be at home with family and a few close friends. Although the wedding was simple, as the bride and groom requested, it was incredibly beautiful.

White and yellow roses tied with dark pink ribbons wrapped around the gazebo's columns. Lit lanterns lined the pathway from the house to the barn. Catherine was the flower girl. Evelyn and Emily's best friend, Betty, were the bride's attendants. Emily had asked Rachel to stand with her, more out of obligation to her mother than a true desire for herself. Rachel refused and attended the wedding only at her father's ardent demand.

Simon Garrett, Betty's brother, was John's best man, Sam and William groomsmen. Betty Garrett Lovelace, who had married in January, was Emily's matron of honor. Betty wore a peach chiffon dress. Long peach ribbons descended from her wide-brimmed ivory hat. Evelyn and Catherine wore matching pastel yellow dresses. A large white satin bow was tied perfectly in the back. Each carried a white basket filled with yellow roses and pink carnations. John, as well as his groomsmen, looked handsome in their light grey three-piece pin-striped suits.

Sitting on the front row, Maggie held Franklin's hand as she watched John waiting for his bride to appear. John's face beamed when Emily, escorted by her father, walked slowly down the aisle towards him. She looked radiant in her ankle length white satin slim-fitting gown. An overlay of Tulle lace provided modesty over the low-cut bodice. The veil of Chantilly lace fell from the back of Emily's head to the middle of her back. She borrowed her mother's white pearl choker and wore new white pumps. A train, attached at her shoulders, flared out in a puddle of cascading ivory lace. It whooshed on the grass as she walked.

Reaching the end of the aisle, Mr. Moore placed Emily's hand within John's. The bride and groom turned to face Reverend Collins. John helplessly fought back tears. Rachel, sitting across the aisle on the first row by her mother also stifled tears, but hers were not sparked by happiness.

All the family on both sides plus close friends—the Carsons, the Jeters, and the Lawrences— attended. Everyone except Art. He remained at the King Ranch. Although his feelings had not changed, he sent a telegram, addressed to John only, extending best wishes.

The party that followed the wedding ceremony was certainly comparable to the barbecue a year before. There were just fewer guests. The musicians, as on cue, began to play as John and Emily entered the marked off area for dancing.

Earlier Emily had removed her veil and train for easier movement at the reception. John led his bride to the center of the grass. He spun her around and pulled her close for their first dance together as a married couple. She held tightly to the back of his arm, crushing his suit jacket in her fingers. They moved easily and slowly to the rhythm of the music. They gazed into each other's eyes, as if they were the only couple there. Other couples began to dance as the fiddles and guitars played.

"May I say, Mrs. Bailey, how breathtaking you look," John whispered.

"Mrs. Bailey. Is that my name now?" Emily teased.

As the instruments played "Always" by Irving Berlin, John sang softly against Emily's ear. "I'll be loving you always. With a love that's true always….That's when I'll be there always. Not for just an hour, not just a day. Not for just one year, but always…"

As the next song began, Emily's father asked to dance with his daughter. Emily, tears in her eyes and a smile on her face, took her father's hand.

John saw his father talking to Fred Jeter and Jim Carson by one of the tables. He joined them. Fred and Jim, both, wished him well. They exclaimed what a lovely bride he had before excusing themselves to find their wives for a dance.

Franklin patted John on the back. "Santos and Tia will be gone to South Texas for a couple of weeks and offered their home to you and Emily."

"Oh, swell! Thank them for me, for us. Yes, we'll take it. We were just going to Austin for the night. This is great! Couldn't plan a honeymoon. Emily has only a couple of days before she must get back. We'd hoped to stay here until we leave for Galveston."

"Of course, have you found a position there, son?"

"Not yet, but I have some promising leads."

"Your mom is trying to get our attention. Must be time to cut the cake."

I love weddings, don't you? The traditional wedding celebration—wedding cake consumption, toasts of champagne, dancing under the stars, wedding gifts, laughter and gaiety, claps on the back, kisses on the cheeks, tears, congratulations, and best wishes—continued several more hours. With the fiddles and guitars finally encased, one more round of hugs commenced before the guests departed.

"It's been a long day. I've got to get the girls to bed. It was a beautiful wedding. I'm happy for you both," Maggie kissed Emily on the cheek and hugged her son.

John and Emily stood near the gazebo and watched the Bailey family walk up the path to the house. "You look tired," he said.

"My feet hurt! Why do women dance in heels?"

"It's late, Emmy. We can change clothes and drive to Austin to the hotel or we can stay in the cottage."

Emily looked over his shoulder toward the cottage. "Hmm, I don't know. Can we look at it first?"

"Of course." He took her hand. She diverted her eyes as they walked down the path, past the corral, past the barn, and past the garden.

John turned the knob and pushed the door open. "Wait! Let me find the oil lamps."

Emily stood in the doorway and waited until the lamp emitted a sudden bright beam, lighting the room. She stepped through the threshold and surveyed the three-room house. It was cozy and clean which would be expected since Tia lived there. A sofa, with a red and green and gold serape blanket draped over its back, faced the limestone fireplace. A rocking chair sat to one side of the sofa. A woven basket filled with colorful balls of yarn sat near it on the floor. Piles of chopped wood kept in a wood box sat on one side of the hearth. A guitar leaned against the other. An oak table and four wicker-back chairs sat in the center of the room. A bowl of freshly cut flowers centered the table.

The kitchen, a small space in the great room, held a small cabinet with a sink, a wood burning stove and an ice box. An oak china cabinet with four drawers and three shelves lined with stoneware sat against the wall leading to the bedroom. In the opposite corner of the great room, a black intricately cut tooled leather saddle sat proudly displayed on a saddle rack. Silver floral conchos accented the entire housing. Ornamental silver stirrups were well-polished. Initials, "T.S," were engraved in the leather on the pommel and down the fenders.

The bedroom held a four-poster bed, an armoire, and an upholstered green floral chair. A coal lamp was placed on the nightstand. A vanity dresser, with an oval mirror and red upholstered stool, completed the room. The third room, Ernie had added, was an indoor toilet, complete with a clawfoot tub.

"What do you think? What do you want to do?"

"It's so quaint and I'm so tired. That bathtub looks so inviting."

"Ok, but first, come here." John swooped Emily up in his arms and carried her back out through the front door.

"I think it's supposed to be the other way," she laughed.

"Fine," he put her down on the stoop and kissed her. Before she could say anything, he swooped her up again and entered the house. He carried her to the bedroom and positioned her standing, facing him.

He moved closer and touched her face and her hair. "Mrs. Bailey, I think you need help with all these buttons and lace."

She smiled coyly. "You may be correct, Mr. Bailey."

He moved behind her. He removed the choker from her neck and placed it on the vanity. He began to unbutton the tiny buttons down the back of her dress. The dress became loosened enough to slide off her shoulders. Emily grabbed one side.

"Uh, uh, my job," he playfully slapped at her hands.

She let the dress fall in a crumpled mound of satin and lace at her feet. He moved around to face her and helped her step from the dress. He gathered it up from the floor and carefully laid it across the arms of the chair in the corner. Emily shivered, out of nervousness more than a sudden chill. She wore a satin chemise slip that fell below her knees. John led her to the stool at the vanity and she sat down. He knelt beside her and lifted her right foot to his knee. He unbuckled her shoe and let it drop to the floor. He massaged her toes and then untied the blue ribbon that held her hosiery in place. He rolled it from her leg and continued the process with her left foot.

John pulled her up and kissed her mouth, then covered her neck and earlobes with kisses. She closed her eyes. He gently pulled one strap over her arm and kissed her neck. When the chemise began to slide down, he whispered her name. Emily suddenly opened her eyes and grabbed at the cloth, frantically covering herself.

John looked startled.

"Oh, John, I'm sorry, but I…I'd like to bathe. I'm so sweaty from dancing and from all the activities today. Would you mind getting my overnight bag from the car, sweetheart? I'd like a change of clothes, too."

"Of course, Emily," he paused, puzzled, "is everything okay?"

"Yes, of course, I…I just…I…want everything to be perfect." Standing on tiptoes, she hurriedly kissed him then rushed to the bathroom and closed the door.

After bathing, Emily appeared in the doorway. John was waiting for her in bed, leaning against the pillows. The quilt lay folded at the foot of the bed. The linens were pulled to his waist. John watched as she approached his side of the bed. She turned down the lamp wick as John held up a corner of the sheet and moved over. She slipped underneath and lay her head against his chest.

The house was dark as pitch, except for the dim moonlight streaming from the window. The room was as quiet as newly fallen snow. John held his bride for a few minutes, feeling her heartbeat against his skin. He gently pulled his fingers through her long curly hair and then pulled her up to kiss her. This time she responded without reservation.

After making love, she fell asleep. John could not. As the moonlight glowed through the window, he leaned upon an elbow and watched her sleep. She was so beautiful. Her copper hair splayed out on the pillow like a fan. He watched her chest rise and fall so peacefully with each breath. She lay on her back with her arms resting on top of the linens. Her skin was as soft as velvet; she was perfection. He laid back on his pillow and placed his left arm over his head. He knew he was undoubtedly the luckiest man in the world. He had patiently waited for her and her love. God had certainly blessed him.

But what was it she had murmured when they were making love? Her voice had been so hushed and low. Had he misunderstood? Surely, it was not what he imagined. It couldn't be, could it? No, he was not mistaken; he'd heard plainly, undeniably. Emily was whispering another man's name; she was pining for his brother.

GOOD NEWS BAD NEWS

FALL 1929

In the early weeks of September 1929, Franklin came home from work at his regular hour. Unlike his customary routine of seeing Maggie first, he went straight to his study. He tossed two items on his desk. The current edition of the *Austin Tribune* and a letter he had received, opened, and read several times earlier at work. He had decided on his drive home, he would tell Maggie after dinner about the letter and the phone call he had received from John.

Dinner time, a customary routine, was bristling with activity and teeming with savory aromas. Franklin pushed open the kitchen door. Maggie greeted him warmly, patting his cheek as she kissed him. She quickly returned to the stove to stir the gravy. Clay and Paddy set the dining room table with the every-day blue floral china. The white china was reserved for Sundays. Sam and Willie brought side dishes in from the kitchen and placed them in the center of the table.

"Hey, Papa," the boys greeted, almost simultaneously.

Lucy and Loraine, sitting in their highchairs at the dining room table, squealed delightedly when they saw their daddy. Lucy banged her hands against the tray and Loraine kicked her feet in excitement. Franklin kissed them each on the forehead and rustled the younger boys' hair. He patted Sam on the back.

"Evening, Mr. Bailey," Tia greeted, placing the platter of roast beef and the carving knife in front his plate at the head of the table. "I'll be heading home now. Good night, la familia."

"Good night, Tia," Franklin and Maggie answered. The boys waved.

After all the serving dishes were placed on the table and everyone took their seats, Franklin offered grace. In his prayer, he asked God to bless the food, to protect his family and to guide the nation. Maggie lifted her head quizzically, wondering what he meant but would save her questions for later.

After reading a story to Clay and Paddy, Franklin tucked the younger boys in bed. He joined Sam first in his room and then Willie in his. He sat down on the edge of Willie's bed and listened to him share about his day. Tip lay curled at the end of the bed. The dog sat up as Franklin stood. He patted Tip on the head and wished his son a good night's sleep. He turned down the wick on the oil lamp and left the room, closing the door behind him.

He entered his bedroom. Peaches, curled on a rug in front of the unlit fireplace, wagged her tail. Maggie was in bed propped against two pillows nursing Loraine. Loraine kicked her legs when she heard him enter. Franklin crawled on top of the covers toward Maggie and took his daughter's hand in his. He stroked her blonde baby curls as Loraine gripped his fingers.

"You are beautiful. You do you know that don't you?"

"Are you talking to me or Loraine?"

Franklin kissed his wife. "You, of course."

"Ha! I feel like Glo, our cow! Why has this little girl been so stubborn about being weaned? Lucy was so easy. Do you realize I've been tied to these two little calves for almost two years?"

Franklin smiled then laid back on his pillow, waiting for Loraine to fall asleep. When the baby was finally still, he got up. Maggie readjusted her night dress as Franklin scooped Loraine into his arms and carried her to her crib.

When he returned to their room, he extended his hand, "Maggie, come sit with me on the veranda."

Maggie slipped on a housecoat, and they moved to the rocking chairs on the veranda. Peaches followed and curled next to Maggie's chair. The night, even though it was mid-September, was hot and muggy with only an occasional breeze. Any breeze was welcoming. Before Maggie took a seat, Franklin took her hand and kissed the top of her fingers.

"I love you very much, Maggie. You're a wonderful mother. I don't tell you often enough."

"But you do every day! What's going on, Franklin? What do you want to tell me?"

Franklin finally sat in one of the chairs, Maggie the other. "All day I've been trying to think how to tell you this. There's so much news! I don't know where to start!"

"You're scaring me, Franklin. Just tell me."

"Okay," he swallowed. "Today the *Austin Tribune* reported a financial expert by the name of Roger Babson predicted a Stock Market crash is coming and claimed it may be terrific. The American economy is in trouble. Banks and investors and businesses that speculated heavily have a risk of losing everything. John called me from work and said his job is unstable. If there is a run on the bank, as rumor has it, and the bank closes, he will lose his position. Some of the larger banks will survive. The smaller ones will not. He's worried but not without hope. He would be foolish to search for another precarious bank position now and cannot leave Galveston while Emily is in school. She has one more year of basics then two years of clinical training. He knows he could find a job as a druggist assistant after working with me so many years. He plans to go back to school to get his pharmaceutical license after Emily finishes."

"Oh, Franklin! Are we okay?"

"Yes, Ernie and I did not overly invest in the bank. Folks still need medicine. Our businesses are fine. Don't worry about that." Franklin squeezed Maggie's hands. "There's more."

Maggie's eyes widened as Franklin, not releasing her hands, continued. "I also received a letter from Lorna. As you know, Boise City and, well most of the Oklahoma and Texas plains, have been severely affected by a drought. Their wheat crop may not bring enough money to buy next year's seeds for planting. If things continue to worsen, she and Wilson are asking if Mom and Claudia may come here to stay until things there are better. Susan suffered severely with asthma. They've already sent her to Beaumont to live with Gavin and his wife, Cora. Bless them, they've only been married a year.

Gavin is doing well working on Spindletop Hill. I remember reading in the newspaper about the big gusher. The Lucas Geyser spewed mud, followed by natural gas and oil, 150 feet in the air. That was twenty some years ago. Spindletop is still producing oil! Anyway, Alex is serving in the Army Air Forces. Lorna didn't mention where's he's stationed now."

"Oh, Franklin, how terrible!" Maggie stood, turning to face him. "And John and Emily! I'm not that worried about them. They have us and George and Peg to help them financially. But for John to start school again is just too much. Of course, your mother and Claudia can come here for however long they need. What about all those people who will lose their jobs? Or have little income? Or will lose everything they've worked so hard for? What will they do? This is all so dreadful!"

Franklin rose and took his wife into his arms. He placed one hand on the back of her head and pulled her gently toward him. She buried her head against his shoulder as they held each other tightly.

"Mama? They're here! They're here!" Clayton and Paddy shouted, running down the hall. They blasted into the music room.

Maggie was turning pages for Evelyn Moore as she played Beethoven's "Moonlight Sonata." Looking up, Evelyn lifted her fingers from the keyboard. Paddy and Clay stomped about, almost dancing a jig, around Maggie's chair. Maggie nodded and the boys raced from the room. Lucy and Loraine were sitting on the rug in front of the sofa. Their legs splayed out, shoes touching, were playing with their Raggedy Ann dolls.

"Come on, girls, let's go see Granma and Claudia. Evelyn, come along, too. Claudia is your age and will be in your class in school. You can help her get acquainted with your friends."

The twins bounded from the floor, leaving their dolls abandoned on the rug. Evelyn followed Maggie and the toddlers down the hallway. Franklin stood in the foyer with a suitcase under each arm. His mother stood to his left, Claudia to his right. William stood behind them with two suitcases at his feet.

In their excitement, Clay and Paddy almost tackled their grandmother. The twins hid behind their mother. Lucy clutched Maggie's skirt on one side. Holding on to her mother's skirt on the other side, Loraine sucked her first two fingers. They peered around and watched their brothers curiously. Claudia stepped back out of the way but had nowhere to hide.

Claudia looked younger than her fifteen years, Maggie thought. But that was probably due to her dress. The blue cotton print with tiny, dark blue flowers fell like a sack from her shoulders. Indeed, it was a sack, a flour sack. A matching blue belt gathered the loosely fitted dress about her waist. The puffy sleeves touched her elbows. The edge of the dress dropped a few inches above her ankles. Her worn laced-up boots needed polish. Claudia's blonde plaited hair fell in a single braid over her right shoulder. The brim of her red felt cloche hat shaded an astounding color of green eyes.

Maggie noticed Claudia's and Evelyn's appraisal of each other. Evelyn offered a friendly smile. Claudia, blank-faced, self-consciously adjusted her belt and eyed the girl up and down. The girl wore a soft pink sheer rayon dress. The tiered collar flowed over capped sleeves. The dress hugged the girl's slim body. Pleats flared out slightly below her knees. A white leather belt with two dollar-sized white pearl buttons in its center wrapped around the girl's small waist. The girl's stockings shimmered in the light. Her pumps were white with small gold buckles. A white ribbon held the girl's dark brunette hair away from her face. Curls fell to the top of her shoulders. Claudia, eyes casted downward, rubbed the toe of her right boot behind the back of her left.

"Momma Bailey," Maggie kissed her mother-in-law's cheek. "Welcome."

"Maggie, my dear. We don't know how to thank you. Your children have grown so. Look at them! No longer babies. Do you mind if I lie down? It was a long train ride. Can we visit later?"

"Of course, freshen up and rest. Sam is at work and will be home for dinner. Claudia, William will you show you to your room. This way, Momma. Clay and Paddy, take your sisters out to the porch to ride their rocking horse. Evelyn, Franklin will take you home as soon as his mother is settled."

"Of course," Franklin agreed, smiling at Evelyn.

"Thank you," Evelyn replied, watching the strange girl climb the stairs.

William took the lead up the stairs carrying two suitcases. Claudia trailed silently behind. Maggie held Momma Bailey's arm as they ascended the stairs. Franklin followed with his mother's suitcases. As Claudia turned onto the landing, she looked down at the girl in pink. Evelyn smiled and waved but Claudia was still unresponsive.

As William entered Art's old room, he placed the cases on the floor in front of the bed. "Are these okay here?" He looked up as Claudia plucked her hat from her head. She shrugged and sat on the edge of the bed, clutching her hat as she looked around the room.

Franklin, seeing his mother was settled down for a nap, came out on the porch. "Ready to go, Evie?"

Evelyn nodded and stood from where she'd been watching the boys build a bridge with their Tinker Toys. Maggie, having returned from upstairs, sat in a rocking chair watching the twins. The toddlers were rocking happily in the rocking horse.

Ernie had built it using oak scraps. The girls sat together on a wooden seat inside the box. The box was secured to two rockers. A wooden bar for them to hold stretched across the chair. A horse head cutout was attached on either side of the box. A white tail made of dyed straw was fastened onto the back. The chair was painted pink with big white spots. Oh, how the girls loved that rocking horse.

"Please tell your mother I'll invite her soon for tea. I hope to see you next week. Give my best to Cat. Sorry, she was not feeling well." Maggie stood to pat Evelyn's back. "You're doing so well on the sonata."

Evelyn waved as Franklin opened the pickup door for her.

"Paddy, you two, watch the girls. I'm going up to check on Claudia," Maggie instructed.

"Yes, 'em," Paddy replied as he and Clay continued to build their bridge.

As Maggie neared Claudia's room, she heard crying. Maggie knocked gently on the door. "Claudia, may I come in?"

When there was no response, Maggie pushed the door open gently. Her niece was curled in a ball on the edge of the bed. Maggie sat down beside her. Claudia sat up. Her eyes were red from crying.

"Oh, sweet thing," Maggie drew the girl into her arms. "This must be extremely hard for you. Coming here and being away from your parents. They thought being here was best under the circumstances. I hope that we can make you feel most welcome. Because you are family, we want you to know you belong."

Claudia sniffled, "Everything here is lovely. So green! So clean! So much different from home. I just don't fit in. Look at me!" She stood from the bed and pulled at her dress. "This is horrible! On the train today I heard women whispering to each other that Granma and I must be Okies! So rude! I felt so small and well, ugly! Look at this dress! The girl downstairs was splendid! She was wearing heaven! I've never owned anything but scratchy cotton and ole hand-me-down denim overalls."

Maggie pulled Claudia to the full-length mirror stand she had insisted Franklin move from their bedroom. "Look at yourself in the mirror. You are a beauty. Clothes and origins, where we come from, don't define who we are. Your inner beauty makes your outer beauty shine through. If you'd like I can ask Uncle Franklin to bring a Sears, Roebuck Catalog from town. We can pick out a few dresses and a couple pairs of shoes to order for you. Until the shipment comes, maybe one of my friends might have dresses their daughters have outgrown and no longer wear. How does that sound?"

Claudia turned and wrapped her arms around Maggie's neck. "Thank you so much! If I'll look like that pink girl, I'll be happy!"

Maggie laughed, "That pink girl's name is Evelyn Moore. Your cousin John is married to her eldest sister, Emily. Evelyn is your age. It's possible you two will become dearest of friends."

"More tea, Jewel?" Maggie asked as she held up a rose print tea pot. "I'm so thrilled you all could come this afternoon to meet Momma Bailey."

"No, thank you," Jewel Jeter shook her head. "This is lovely, Maggie. I love getting away from my regular day. Having the chance to meet you, Mrs. Bailey, is a delight. We've heard so much about you."

Peg Moore and Letty Carson nodded in agreement. The five ladies sat at a round table in the parlor. It was a school day so none of the children were under foot. Tia had taken the twins with her to the garden to pick flowers. The windows were opened to allow fresh air to fill the room.

"Oh, you are all so kind. Please, just call me Bessie. My son found the prize in Maggie here." Bessie patted the top of her daughter-in-law's hand. "I'm grateful to be here. Things just got so bad, that's all. Couldn't imagine them getting worse in Boise City, but they sure did. Lorna and Wilson, my daughter and son-in-law, just won't call it quits. That farm has been in Wilson's family for generations. Many farmers and their families, practically poverty-stricken, were forced to leave. It was just so hard." Bessie's voice slightly broke.

Peg Moore waited for Bessie to recover. "What happened? Would you tell us?"

Bessie took a sip of her tea then smiled. "Of course. We have lived through droughts before. Were familiar with them, a part of farm life. But after such long spells without rain, the crops died. We made a bumper crop of wheat the year before. Wheat prices were high, and the future seemed prosperous. We had no idea things would be, could be, so bad this year. Without corn or wheat, Wilson couldn't feed the livestock. He was finally able to sell the healthy cows and stock to a farmer in Texas but didn't make much. No one has much money these days. The dust storms…," Bessie hesitated. The ladies, captivated by her story, were eager for her to continue.

"We were used to dust storms, too, but these were monsters! Devils! The sound was deafening. Sounded like howling, no more like roaring. The rolling, choking dirt, and the smell! I'll never forget it! The sand would sift under the doors and windowsills no matter how many rags or blankets were stuffed under them. Everything was covered with a fine powder. You'd go to bed at night and wake up with an outline of fine dirt framing your head on the pillow. Poor Lorna tried to keep the house clean, but it was impossible. She'd wipe down the tables and chairs and even the walls with a wet rag. She couldn't leave any food uncovered. Dirt is not tasty!" Bessie laughed and the ladies echoed warily.

"We heard tell that some places were harder hit than ours. One farmer said he couldn't get out of his house one morning. The sand had settled like a dune barricading his front door and windows. He had to climb out the back window and shovel away the dirt from the front of the house. Didn't do any good, though; it would come right back. It always did. Any bit of wind would bring a raging wall of sand. Static electricity built up between the ground and the airborne dust sparking blue flames from barbed wire fences. Wilson tied a fifty-foot rope from the porch railing to the barn door just in case he was caught out in the storm and couldn't see to get back to the house. Oh, and poor Claudia and Susan. The kids, even the boys, had to wear scarves over their faces and goggles over their eyes when they went outside or walked to school. Their hats had to be secured tightly or they'd blow away! I often wonder how many hats were found over in the next county!" Bessie chuckled.

"The girls wore thick socks under their dresses or wore overalls to protect their legs from the stinging bite of grit. And sometimes it was hard to distinguish day from night. The sky was so dark. I got kinda sick with what the doctor called dust pneumonia. A lot of babies and older folks from our community died…just couldn't breathe! So tragic! That's when Wilson and Lorna said enough was enough and sent us here. I'm much better now that I can breathe clean air!"

"And how is Claudia faring?" Peg asked after taking a small bite of a sugar cookie and placing the rest on her dessert plate.

"She seems to be doing fine," Bessie replied. "Thanks to your girl. Evelyn has been most kind."

"That reminds me," Maggie interjected. "Sam and Willie have invited their friends over Saturday to meet Claudia. Sort of a welcoming party. I know Rachel is working at the newspaper office with her dad. I was hoping Evelyn and Cat, and your girls, Letty, could come. My nephews Harold and Owen are coming, too."

"Of course," Peg said. "Evelyn had already mentioned it."

"I'm sure Mary and Constance would love to come," Letty added.

"Oh, my girls are so much older than yours, but sounds like a fun time," Jewel added, reaching for another cookie.

"Wonderful! Bring them around by 2:00 p.m. Elizabeth is taking Clay and Paddy and the twins with her to play with Carter. This will be a nice outing for the young people."

CHOICES AND CHANCES

SPRING ** SUMMER 1930

Claudia, trying to make sense of the rules, sat to one side of the card table set on the wide wrap-around porch for the "42" domino players. Sam and his friend, Leo Manor, had challenged Trina and Evelyn to a match, best two out of three.

"It's your bid, Trina," Evelyn announced, watching Trina study her dominoes.

"Time's ticking," Sam teased, drumming his fingers on the table.

"Ok, ok. I bid 32. Fours are trumps."

"That's outstanding, solid!" Evelyn exclaimed, rearranging the dominos lined in front of her.

"Is that considered talking across the table?" Leo asked, evidently annoyed.

The competition between the sexes was comical, Claudia mused as she looked out on the lawn. Mary and Constance Carson were playing badminton against Harold Foster, Ernie's stepson, and Sam's school chum, Charlie Spooner. The net had been set up earlier that morning. Cat sat cross-legged on the grass waiting her turn to play. Mary served the birdie, or shuttlecock as called by its proper name, and eyed it hopefully as it sailed lopsidedly over the net. Harold swung his racket low catching the birdie in the middle of his racket's strings and lobbed it back to the girls' court. Constance advanced to the net excitedly but swung her racket as if swatting a fly. She watched disappointedly as the birdie fell at her feet. The boys congratulated themselves with high-fives.

On the other side of the lawn, Owen and Willie were playing catch, urging each other to throw the baseball harder and higher. The sound of the thump as each fielded ball hit the baseball glove merged almost musically with the sounds of the shuffling of dominoes and the whacking of shuttlecocks.

Claudia, bored from watching the domino and lawn games, glanced to her right. A tall young man dressed in a blue cotton shirt, denim jeans and black boots sat leaning against the limestone column. His long legs, crossed at the ankles, rested along the edge of the porch. Earlier Sam had introduced him as one of his coworkers from Bond Construction. They had worked together for several months. Claudia studied him. He was indeed a handsome fellow. His hair was dark, almost black. She watched as a he often pushed a strand of hair dangling across his forehead to one side. His eyes, too, were dark, his lashes long. His forearms were muscular, and his body fit. He looked older, but Claudia didn't care. He seemed interesting and was most appealing to the eye. She rose from her chair and walked toward him. He sat upright placing his feet on the ground as she sat down next to him.

"Alan, right?"

He smiled a lopsided grin, "And you're Claudia."

"You're not from around here either, are you?"

"No, I'm from Childress. Ever heard of it?"

She smiled and shook her head no. She reached for his hand. He obligingly surrendered it and watched as she turned it over to examine his palm. "Callouses are signs of hard work. My dad's hands are calloused." She slowly traced the thickened skin with her finger. "He always said a man's hands says everything you needed to know about the man."

She released his hand and leaned back on her elbows. "It's too beautiful a day to just sit on this stuffy porch!"

She suddenly sprang up on the edge of the porch and kicked off her shoes. She pulled her blue chambray skirt up over her knees and rolled down her stockings from first her right leg, then her left. Alan, spellbound, watched her. Noticing Claudia's behavior, Trina nudged Evelyn's foot with her shoe. She motioned her head toward Claudia. Turning to look, Evelyn's eyes widened with shock.

Claudia stuffed her stockings into her skirt pockets and grabbed Alan's hands, pulling him up. "Let's go swing!"

"Hey! Look out!" Willie shouted as an overthrown ball whizzed past Alan's head.

"Throw it back, Alan," Owen positioned his glove ready to retrieve the ball.

Claudia laughed as she hip-bumped Alan out of the way. She scooped up the ball, turned and threw it straight into Owen's glove.

Owen was surprised and impressed. "Wow! Thanks, Claudia. You've got quite an arm! Here, Willie, catch! I may trade partners if you can't control your throw."

Willie caught the ball and grimaced back.

"I have two older brothers," Claudia responded to Alan's quizzical look.

Claudia slipped her hand under Alan's arm, holding tightly, as they neared the rope swing. She grasped the two ropes on either side of the wooden seat and sat down. As she walked the swing backwards, Alan grasped her around the waist. He held her for a few seconds, then released her. She squealed each time he pushed her forward. As he pushed her higher, she extended her legs and pointed her toes. She seemed clearly unconcerned when the air currents caught her skirt and lifted it over her knees.

"How old is he anyway, Sam?" Trina asked as Leo shuffled the dominoes for the next game.

"What?" Sam turned his attention to Trina's pointing finger. "Oh, Alan? He's twenty; a good guy. Been working for Uncle Ernie for six months. A really hard worker."

"Claudia is my age! Only fifteen!" Evelyn protested.

"Ahh, he's okay. Won't be around long. Alan and I will be going to Mason the end of May. Uncle Ernie won a bid to build a bank there. We'll be gone several months."

"What? You didn't tell me!" Trina, pouting her bottom lip, looked heartbroken. "You're leaving after graduation and will be gone all summer?"

Sam placed his hand on top of hers, "I was going to tell you tonight. I…"

Tia opened the front door, "Sandwiches and lemonade are waiting at the gazebo. Please, help yourselves."

The mood in the gazebo was lively. Chicken salad finger sandwiches, slices of home canned peaches, and strawberry cake mastered everyone's appetite. The rest of the afternoon was teeming with gaiety, laughter amid jokes and teasing. Arguments arose over which film was better Buster Keaton's comedy film, "Steamboat Bill, Jr." or the romantic drama, "Show Boat." As the afternoon progressed, Mary and Constance Carson, Cat Moore, Leo Manor and Harold Foster were the first guests to leave.

"Hey! Let's go to the creek!" Willie suggested, after shoveling down another sandwich.

Sam and Trina, Evelyn and Charlie, and lastly Alan and Claudia paired off. The couples followed Willie and Owen to the creek. Finding a shady oak tree, Evelyn shook out the green plaid blanket Tia left at the gazebo. She knelt on it, flattening the corners with her hands. Charlie, Claudia, and Alan joined her on the blanket. Sam led Trina a few feet away for a private conversation. Willie and Owen skimmed rocks across the water. Enjoying conversation and time with each other, no one was aware of the hour. The sun, casting deeper shadows under the already shaded trees, began to slip lower in the western horizon's grip.

"How cold is the water this time of year?" Claudia asked.

"It's cold! Believe me!" Sam replied, leading Trina to the blanket.

"Hmmm, let's see." Claudia jumped to her bare feet and walked to the edge of the water. She stuck her toes in the water and wriggled them about.

"Not that bad," she said as she untucked her blouse and began to quickly unbutton the buttons. With her blouse off, she pulled down her skirt and stepped out of it. The two garments lay trampled beneath her feet. Wearing only a white rayon full slip, Claudia faced her stunned audience.

"Come on! Who's with me?"

"Claudia!" Trina shrieked.

Claudia walked briskly to the middle of the creek, splashing animatedly. She sat down letting the frigid water roll over her shoulders. She bobbled around a couple of times, only her head exposed. She faced the onlookers and laughed as she kicked her legs, splashing water their direction.

Evelyn shooed everyone off the blanket and pulled it from the ground. She held it out in front of her as she neared the edge of the water. "Sam, get her out of there!"

"Claudia, come on, now. It's getting late and I know that water is colder than you're letting on." Sam said, sternly, standing on the bank.

Claudia grinned impishly, ducked under the water then stood up. Water trickled down her body as she walked toward the others. Her slip hugged her body, clinging to her every swell and curve. Evelyn and Trina held the blanket up and Claudia let them pull it around her shoulders. All the while she kept eye contact with Alan. Sam and Charlie averted their eyes respectfully, but Willie and Owen were transfixed.

"I can't believe you did that!" Evelyn exclaimed.

Trina picked up Claudia's clothes and followed Evelyn and Claudia up the slope. As they neared where Alan was standing under a tree, Claudia pulled away. Evelyn stumbled behind holding the blanket out as if trying to catch a butterfly in a net.

"Meet me here at midnight," Claudia whispered to Alan.

As Claudia turned to return to her captors, Willie was staring at her. Evelyn, with Trina's assistance this time, secured the blanket around her. Both Evelyn and Trina were determined to get this mischievous girl back to the house safely. Since Alan had offered Charlie a ride, Sam walked with them to Alan's truck parked in the driveway. Owen and Willie raced to the house, whether they would blurt out what had happened, no one knew.

"I can't believe your behavior all day! You're shameless!" Evelyn scolded as the girls reached the back outer stairs.

Claudia laughed, "And you're a pansy, no doubt! A little wallflower! Dull! I bet you've never been kissed!"

"What? Of course, I have!" Evelyn protested.

"Boys don't count!"

"Come on, Evelyn," Trina coaxed, as she shoved Claudia's clothes at her. "This is ridiculous!"

Evelyn dropped the blanket at Claudia's feet and glared at her. She and Trina walked hurriedly around to the front of the house searching for Sam.

Claudia grabbed the blanket and scrambled up the back stairs to the veranda. She ran to her room and closed the door behind her. She threw her skirt and blouse on the bed and grabbed a towel from the chifforobe to dry her arms and legs. She pulled off her slip and rolled it tightly into the towel to dry. She stood in front of the full-length mirror. Her wet hair was plastered to her head and neck. Dribbles of water dripped onto her shoulders and slid down her chest. Goosebumps marched up and down her cold skin. She leaned in closely, blinking her eyelashes, and pouting her lips. Smiling, she stepped back. She put her hands on her waist. Turning to the right and then the left, she studied her reflection.

"You are mine, Alan Woods," she whispered.

After dressing for dinner, Claudia joined the family downstairs. She was bombarded by questions from the adults about the party. She answered graciously how wonderful the day had been. Sam and Willie, she noticed gratefully, did not comment. She ate quickly and, feinting a headache, excused herself from the table.

She returned to her room, opened the doors to the veranda, and sat down on the floor. She leaned against her bed and listened as the clock on her desk tick-ticked away the hours. It was dark outside. The time piece seemed to persistently dawdle away the last hour on purpose, delaying her rendezvous with Alan.

"Claudia?" Granma knocked softly at the door.

Claudia scrambled into bed, fully dressed, and pulled the covers to her neck. She rolled on her side, squinched her eyes closed and pretended to sleep. She heard the door open, and her grandmother approach the bed.

"Sleep well, my dear," Granma whispered, patting her granddaughter's shoulder.

Claudia lay like a bedpost until she was sure Granma was no longer in the room. She bounded from the bed and stood in front of the mirror. She had tried on three dresses before deciding the one she was wearing was perfect. The dress, one of her favorites, was a light green floral rayon with a flowing gathered skirt. She opted to only wear her sheer lacy chemise bandeau bra and matching tap pants underneath. As the clock's hands moved to ten minutes until midnight, Claudia slipped her stockingless feet into her shoes. She examined herself once more in the mirror and then headed out onto the veranda.

She tiptoed down the veranda's corridor, past the other bedrooms, her ears pricked for sounds. When she took the fourth step down the stairs, she suddenly stopped. Willie and Tip sat on the steps halfway down.

"What on earth, Willie! You scared me!"

"Yeah? Sorry. So where are you going at this late hour?" He stood up.

"What are you doing out here?"

"Nothing really. Just keeping watch. Ya know, I can snap my fingers and Tip will start barking. Papa will wonder what you're up to. Want me to show ya?" Willie poised his fingers ready to demonstrate. Tip wagged his tail excitedly.

"No, stop that! You'll wake everyone!"

"Well then, where are you going?"

"Nowhere, just enjoying the night sky and the stars."

"All dressed up like that? You can see the stars better from the veranda. Can you give your word if Tip and I go down to the creek, Alan won't be there?"

"Alan? How would I know where he is? Okay, you win. I'm going back to my room. It's late. You should do the same."

"After you." Willie started up the stairs forcing Claudia to turn around.

Claudia closed her door and leaned against it, listening for Willie and Tip. She had no other choice. She'd have to leave through the house. She opened her bedroom door slowly and stepped into the hallway. She inched toward the main stairs, walking slowly, fearful the floor would creak. She quickly descended the second flight of stairs, the landing, and the first flight. She crossed the foyer to the entry hall and opened the front door. She closed the door quietly behind her and rushed down the porch steps. She ran down the driveway until she reached the road. She glanced to the left and then to the right. To her delight, there to the right, fifty feet from the driveway sat Alan's 1921 Chevrolet Roadster. He was smoking a Camel as he leaned against the side of the pickup, one foot on the running board.

"Hey," Claudia greeted as she approached the truck. "You came."

"Who could turn down an invitation like yours?" Alan turned to face her, grinning his charming, crooked smile. "I waited by the creek. When you didn't show, I came back here. I was going to give you five more minutes before I left."

"Don't leave! I'm sorry I'm late. That punk kid Willie and his dog were on the back stairs threatening to wake Uncle Franklin."

"What now?" Alan snuffed out his cigarette with the toe of his boot.

"I thought we could just talk or look at the stars."

"You did, huh? Say, Sam told me Evelyn and Trina think I'm too old for you."

Claudia stepped upon the running board. "How old do you want me to be?"

Eye to eye with Alan, she gazed into his dark eyes. She pushed the loose strand of hair from his forehead and placed her hands on either side of his face. She kissed him, then dropped her hands to her sides.

"Wow! That's not a little girl's kiss." Alan stepped back.

"I'm not a little girl."

"Yeah, I noticed that at the creek." He snickered.

He cocked his head waiting for her next move. When she remained still, he moved closer placing his hands on either side of her upper arms.

"Kiss me again," he pleaded, pulling her arms around his neck.

After four or five more kisses, each more passionate and fervid than the last, Claudia pushed away. She stepped from the running board, breathing heavily.

"Here," she pulled his hand onto her chest. "Feel my heart pounding? That's what you do to me."

He smiled deviously, "Yeah, sure, I feel it."

Releasing his hand, Claudia asked, "Will you meet me again tomorrow night? I must go now. Willie is probably patrolling around the house."

"Sure, here?"

"No, now that I know Willie is on to us, where else can we go?"

"How about we drive down the road a bit, out of sight, but not too far?"

"I'll bring a blanket to stretch out in the back of your truck. We can explore the stars."

He leaned forward, nibbled at her ear, and whispered, "Whatever you say."

She smiled sheepishly, kissed him goodnight, and retraced her steps to her room.

Oh, Claudia, sweet child, what are you up to?

"I can't believe Sam will be graduating in two weeks!" Maggie declared as she cut pieces of biscuit dough with a tin cutter and placed the rounds on a baking pan.

"It's been a wonderful three months being with your children, Maggie. I've loved getting to know them better," Granma replied.

Tia looked up as Loraine and Lucy skipped into the room. Claudia trailed behind. The girls ran to their mother and twirled around. They wore matching lilac dresses with yellow ribbons tied to the ends of their plaited hair. Holding out their plaits proudly, the twins danced around the kitchen.

It was unnecessary to dress the girls in different colors to tell them apart. But the girls wanted to match anyway. Easily distinguishable, Lucy's hair was brunette and Loraine's blonde. Their blue eyes and facial features were similar. Such darling little things.

"Thank you, Claudia, for fixing their hair this morning. Breakfast will be ready as soon as the biscuits are done."

"I'm not hungry, Aunt Maggie, but thank you. I'm going to my room to wait until Uncle Franklin is ready to take us to school. Will you send Paddy or Clay up when it's time?"

"But you must eat something, Claudia. It's a long time 'til lunchtime," Granma pleaded.

"I'll be okay, Granma." Claudia quickly left the kitchen before being forced to eat.

"Have you noticed how tired she's been lately? Think she's coming down with something?" Granma asked Maggie, thinking Claudia was out of hearing range.

Claudia rushed not to the main stairs to go to her room, but out the front door to the road. Alan's truck was parked in his regular spot waiting for her. Claudia opened the passenger door and scooted into the seat. She leaned across and kissed him good morning.

"What's so important, morning glory? I need to get to work."

"Alan, I need to talk to you. I think…I…. I'm."

Alan lifted her chin when her lips quivered. "What is it? You think you love me?"

"Yes, I do, very much but I'm…oh, Alan."

"Spit it out, cutes. I need to go."

"I'm going to have a baby!"

Alan stared at her hoping he'd misunderstood what she said. When the spiderwebs dusted clear in his head, he hit the steering wheel twice with his fist.

"Impossible! Can't be! I was always careful! You're wrong!"

"No, it's possible. Very possible. I'm not wrong. We're going to have a baby."

"We? Wait a minute!"

Claudia moved toward him needing reassurance and comfort. He pushed her gently away. Claudia's tears becoming more prevalent streaked her youthful face. She reached out for him again. He struck at her hands, pushing them aside.

"Claudia, I need to think about this. Wow! You dropped a big bomb on me, you know? I can't afford much, but I can give you some money, if that's what you need."

"What?" Claudia screeched. "I need you! To marry me and take care of us!"

"Us? Hold on! Get married? Seriously? I start a new job in Mason in two weeks. I can't get married now!"

Claudia continued to cry. Alan pulled her toward him, wrapping his arms around her. "Shh, shh, okay, okay, I'll work something out. Please, stop crying."

He kissed her cheek, and she lifted her face to his. He kissed her mouth; her lips were wet from crying. He held her for a few minutes, thinking.

"I really need to go to work, babe. I'll think of something. I promise."

"Okay, I love you, Alan," Claudia kissed him once more and opened the door to his truck. She walked slowly back to the house as the Roadster sped down the country road, kicking up dirt behind it.

"Pass the salt, there, Clay," Franklin said after tasting his stringed green beans. "Just another week, now, Sam. You'll be graduating and on your way in the world!"

"Yes, sir," Sam mumbled, his mouth full of fried chicken.

"The party plans are well under way," Maggie added. "John and Emily may come if Emily can take a break between sessions."

"Oh, will be so good to see them!" Granma exclaimed. "Haven't seen them in over a year."

"Thanks, Mama. You don't need to have a big party for me! I leave for Mason the day after graduation with Uncle Ernie and the crew."

"Yes, I know, but it's already planned," Maggie laughed.

"Uncle Ernie extended a full-time position, and I've accepted it for now. But I'm really interested in another trade. Power lines are extending from Waco all the way to Ft. Worth, and electricity is already in use in the big cities. Dallas, Waco, Houston, and Austin are only the beginning! With my income from construction, I can take night classes and get an electrical engineering degree at the University of Texas."

"That's wonderful, son. The farmers and those of us living in rural areas would relish the idea of electricity. Wouldn't we, dear?" Franklin glanced at Maggie and then added, "Paddy, stop aggravating your brother."

"Someday," Sam took another bite of chicken and chuckled at his brothers.

The boys scuffled in their seats until Maggie scowled at them, ceasing further horseplay. Claudia pushed her food around her plate with her fork. She was half-way listening to the conversation, wanting to be anywhere but there.

"Oh, and the oddest thing," Sam continued. "Alan Woods, the guy who works with us… you know, you've met him…didn't show up for work today. Left a note on Uncle Ernie's desk that he'd found a better job elsewhere. Didn't even collect his weekly pay. Just up and left. He didn't say anything to me, and I thought we were friends. We were all surprised; just so unlike him."

Claudia's fork slipped through her fingers and clattered against her plate. Turning everyone's attention her way, she placed her napkin on her plate and stood, "Sorry, may I be excused?"

"Of course, are you okay, dear?" Maggie asked, concernedly.

"Yes, sorry," Claudia fled the room avoiding further questions.

Oh, Claudia, you, poor dear thing. What are you going to do now?

"Claudia is not in her room. Have you seen her?" Granma asked an hour later as Maggie placed the clean plates in the china cabinet.

"She's probably out on the porch. She was clearly upset by something tonight. Not to worry, Mama. I'll find her. I was going to read to the girls. Do you mind doing that for me?"

"Of course," Granma Bailey took the back stairs to the twins' bedroom.

Maggie opened the door to the study. Peaches, curled on the rug, raised her head.

"Franklin, Claudia is not in her room. I'm going out to look for her. Your mom is with the twins. Would you check on the boys?"

"Of course, sweetheart," Franklin placed his ledger to one side and stood from behind his desk. "Need help?"

"No, she's probably just homesick and went for a walk."

"Peaches, come," Franklin commanded, and the dog obediently followed.

Maggie went back through the kitchen to the mudroom, grabbing an Eveready flashlight to light her way in the darkness. She stepped out into the night. Tip, tail wagging, bounded up to greet her. She patted the dog's head. He turned to accompany her down the stone path. As Maggie neared the gazebo, she distinctly heard crying. Tip ran ahead and jumped, clearing the three steps into the gazebo. As Maggie entered, she pointed the flashlight around the area. There in the center of the floor Claudia lay curled in a fetal position. Tip was frantically trying to lick her face as she struggled to push him away.

"Claudia! Oh, whatever is the matter?" Maggie knelt as Claudia sat up and wrapped her arms around her aunt's neck.

Maggie held her niece tightly as only a mother knows how to soothe a child. Claudia's tears and sobs flowed freely.

"I'm such a mess! A horrid person! I don't know what to do!"

"Oh, you're not a horrid person. Tell me, sweetheart, what's wrong? Are you homesick?" Maggie brushed Claudia's hair from her face.

Claudia began to cry again. She grabbed Maggie and held on, not wanting to let go. "My parents will hate me!"

"Claudia, your parents could never hate you! Why do you think they would?"

Claudia pulled away from Maggie and sat up. Her skirt was twisted around her legs, her hair a disheveled mangle. Tip eagerly waited for another barrage of kisses. When Maggie scolded the dog, he obediently sat down.

Maggie waited patiently for Claudia to gather her composure.

"Aunt Maggie, I'm going to have a baby! Alan Woods is…was the father."

"Oh, Claudia, how did this…when did this happen?"

"I've been sneaking out of the house since the first day we met. He is so handsome, so strong, so confident, so adventurous. Different from the boys back home. A man not a boy. I couldn't help myself. I love him, and thought he loved me. He said he did, anyway. We never talked about it, but I was sure we'd marry one day. Especially, now. I am wretched! It's all my fault. He's not to blame. I threw myself at him. I knew exactly what I was doing. I'm so ashamed! What am I going to do?"

"Oh, sweetheart, you're not wretched. If fault were charged, it would be against both of you. Not only you. You know, God's love, grace, mercy and forgiveness are infinite, limitless, never ending. He designed a perfect relationship between a man and a woman. It is indeed a marvelous way of expressing love and devotion. His design is for marriage, between a man and his wife. When hearts are unguarded and emotions uncontrolled, these situations can happen. But life is miraculous. God designed that, too. Franklin and I will help you and this new life in any way we can. We love you, Claudia. But your parents need to know."

"Oh, this will break their hearts. I've disappointed them before. I've always been wild and impulsive, but this..." the frightened and brokenhearted girl, began to cry once more. "Now I'll be a disgrace in everyone's eyes. Trina and Evelyn will gloat. Aunt Maggie, please promise me you won't tell anyone! Not even Uncle Franklin! Or especially Granma! She will be so disappointed in me. Please tell no one until I've talked to my mother. I'm not showing yet, please, no one needs to know."

Maggie stood and extended her hand. "Let's get you back to the house and wash your face. I'll keep your secret until we hear from Lorna."

"Maggie? Look who's here!" Franklin found Maggie relaxing in the music room after putting the twins down for a Sunday afternoon nap. The battery-powered radio was softly playing "Someone to Watch Over Me" by George Gershwin.

Maggie looked up as Franklin stepped to one side of the doorway. A tall, handsome young man, tanned from the sun, muscular from hard work, strolled through the door.

"Art!" Maggie rose quickly from her chair and embraced her son. She kissed his mouth and held his face in her hands. "You look wonderful!"

"Sorry, I missed Sam's and Rachel's graduation party. Papa said Sam and Uncle Ernie are in Mason. He told me about Sam's promotion and plans. I'm so proud of him. I have a few days off and thought I'd drive to Mason to see how they're doing after I leave here. You look wonderful, too," Art took Maggie's hand and spun her around. "It's too quiet around here. Where's the noisy crew?"

Franklin laughed, "The girls are napping. The boys are making tortillas with Tia."

Art laughed, "Are Santos and Tia still doing that on Sunday afternoons? Do you mind if I go say hello? I have a letter for them from Gloria, Tia's cousin."

"Of course," Maggie agreed. "You can tell us what's been going on with you after supper."

As Art stepped through the threshold of the music room, he bumped into Claudia.

"What? Claudia, is that you? Tell me it's not so! Why, you've filled out into a beautiful young lady. The last time I saw you, you were just a scrawny kid. Look at you now! Wow! Oh, sorry, is that improper to say, even to a cousin?"

Claudia laughed as she hugged his neck, "You were rather scrawny, too, as I remember."

"Hey, I'm heading out to the stone house to see Santos and Tia. Want to come along? If you haven't tasted Tia's tortillas, you've not lived!"

"Yes, I have, and they are heavenly. May I join you later? I need to talk to Uncle Franklin and Aunt Maggie first."

"Okay, but I can't promise to save any heavenly morsels for you with Clayton and Paddy already down there. See you later," Art waved back at his parents as he left the room.

Claudia timidly remained at the door.

"Come sit down, Claudia, dear," Franklin invited her to sit by Maggie on the sofa. Franklin took a seat across from them.

Claudia, nervously holding her hands in her lap, said, "You know I've talked to my mother again today. Mother's spoken to Gavin. He and Cora have agreed for me to join Susan and come live with them in Beaumont. At least until after the baby is born and I figure out what to do next." Her voice faltered, "She asked if you would buy my train ticket, Uncle Franklin. She promises to pay you back when she can."

"Of course! No need to pay me back, sweetheart. I'll be happy to do it."

"You can't travel alone, Claudia," Maggie added.

"Why, I can go with her," Franklin offered. "I've not seen Lorna's children in years. I've not met Cora either. Would be a treat for me."

"When are you planning to go?"

"Wednesday," Claudia said softly.

"Three days! So soon?" Maggie clasped Claudia's hand, trying not to cry.

"Please, Aunt Maggie," Claudia's voice was filled with fear and remorse. "Just tell the family I am homesick and want to be with my sister. That is the truth, just don't let John know the real reason. Evelyn would find out, and she already despises me. I couldn't bare hearing her say, 'I told you so.' Mother and I agreed Granma should know. I'll tell everyone else about the baby when I'm ready."

"Of course," Maggie and Franklin agreed in unison.

KINGS AND KNAVES

SUMMER 1930**WINTER 1931

That evening after supper, the Bailey family gathered in the study to hear about Art's adventures on the King Ranch. Art sat on the edge of Franklin's desk; his left leg hooked over the corner. Franklin, smoking his pipe, sat in a red floral winged-back chair. Maggie and Granma sat on the black leather sofa. Claudia, sitting in the matching wing-backed chair, held Loraine in her lap. William sat cross-legged on the floor with Tip's head resting on his knee. Clayton, Paddy and Lucy sprawled out on the floor on their tummies. Leaning on bent elbows, the palms of their hands supported their excited faces. Peaches was curled on her favorite spot in front of the hearth. All eyes were fixed on Art.

"As I've told you in my letters, working on the King Ranch is more than I could ever imagine. I've learned so much. I'm grateful to Santos for teaching me about horses, for his words of encouragement and most of all, for his connection to the Ranch. You know, Santos was once part of the Los Kineños, the King's people. He was born in Kingsland. But his great-grandfather, one of the original vaqueros, was from Mexico.

As the story goes Captain Richard King was a steamboat captain during the Civil War. He and his partner purchased a 15,500-acre Mexican land grant in an area known as the Wild Horse Desert. Nothing but wild lands, scrub brush and yucca. This area was once called El Desierto de los Muertos—Desert of the Dead. But the land near the Santa Gertrudis Creek that King focused on was filled with promise. One year there was a drought in Mexico. As a way of survival, the townspeople of this little Mexican village called Cruillas sold all their cattle to Captain King. He must have been a soft-hearted guy for we know he was quite the visionary. Knowing he had deprived them a livelihood, King invited these people to move from Mexico to Texas. He promised them food, shelter, and income if they'd work his ranch. The town they developed was of course called Kingsland. There are generations of Kineños living there still. Captain King's grandson, Bob Kleberg, runs the ranch today. The headquarters, and the Big House, where the Kings live, are also in Kingsland.

Papa, this is quite a diverse operation. Mr. Kleberg follows the family philosophy to 'buy land and never sell.' He partnered with Humble Oil and began oil and gas exploration. And he's been crossbreeding cattle best suited for the climate and terrain in South Texas. This new breed is a cross between Indian Brahman and British Shorthorns. King calls them Santa Gertrudis. They'll eat almost anything and can endure the hot Texas sun. Really, interesting legacy, the Kings. But my love, of course, is the horses!

I work for a wrangler foreman, Juan De Leon. I think he's related to Santos, second or third cousin or some such. I've learned so much from him. He's teaching me to train cutting ponies. With property as vast as the Ranch, you know horses are valuable. A good cow pony is priceless. Oh, and the saddles and tack are breathtaking. The saddles are made at the tannery in Kingsland. Santos worked there as a kid. Anyway, Bob Kleberg bought Old Sorrel as a colt in 1915. What an animal! Beautiful just isn't an adequate description. Old Sorrel has sired some amazing horses."

"And Tia's cousin tells us Señor De Leon has something else of interest to you, I understand," Franklin interjected.

Art's face turned as red as the drapes framing the window behind him.

"Franklin," Maggie scolded.

"Are you gonna tell us about some silly girl?" Clayton protested as Paddy pushed against him.

"It's getting late," Maggie said. "Look, the girls have fallen asleep. And you two ruffians need to get to bed, too," Maggie gently tossed a sofa pillow at the boys, hitting Clayton in the chest.

Jumping up, Clayton gripped the pillow and aimed it at his mother. Willie grabbed the pillow before either of his younger brothers could cause anyone or anything harm.

"A perfect place to stop," Art said, hopping from the desk.

Loraine had fallen asleep. Curled snuggly in Claudia's lap, the child made it difficult for Claudia to move. Franklin pulled his daughter up. Loraine wrapped her legs around him and rested her head on his shoulder.

"Come on, Lucy girl, wake up," Bessie roused Lucy and helped her stand. Lucy turned and raised her arms up toward Claudia. Obligingly, without a second thought, Claudia lifted her cousin to her hip. She followed Granma and Franklin up the main stairway.

Willie braced his two younger brothers in a headlock until they struggled free from his hold. They snickered as they raced to the stairs.

"Good night," Willie bent over to kiss his mother's cheek.

"Good night, son," Maggie reached up and hugged her son tightly. "Love and kisses."

"Love and kisses," he echoed as he left the room.

Maggie patted the leather sofa, inviting Art to join her. "Come finish your story."

Art plopped beside her and smiled broadly. "I know what you want to know."

Maggie elbowed him gently, "In her last letter, Gloria wrote about a Miss Rosa De Leon. Want to tell me about her?"

Art's face once again turned crimson. "Not getting out of this, am I?"

Maggie shook her head and patted his arm.

"Okay, okay, Rosa is Mr. De Leon's youngest child and only daughter. I'd seen her around the stables. She seemed so at ease around horses. Was able to clean stalls, hooves, tack, and ride as well as her four older brothers. She even dressed like her brothers… wide brimmed hats, boots to her knees, jeans, cotton shirts. I didn't talk to her or even act interested 'cause every wrangler in our outfit had eyes for her."

"What's she like?"

"Oh, Mama, she's like a prize Quarter Horse or a champion Thoroughbred. Not that she looks or smells like a horse," Art laughed. "She's just hard to describe. So elegant, noble, and well-formed. Her hair is thick and wavy and touches her waist. Her eyes…her eyes you'd suppose would be dark like her hair. They're not. They're amber, soft gold. They're the most beautiful eyes I've ever seen!

Anyway, I just went about my work until one day she started coming around the corral to watch me train horses. She'd just watch. One minute she'd be there. The next minute I'd look up and she'd be gone. One day as I was working, she approached the corral. She wore a red dress decorated with embroidered yarn of all colors and a pair of black boots. Her hair, rather than being tied back, was flowing freely over her shoulders! Boy! She was even more attractive that day! If that's possible! When I ended the day and was grooming my horse, she came into the barn and started talking to me. She invited me on a trail ride the next day and of course, I accepted. We have the same admiration for horses and can talk for hours. That's all. With her older brothers keeping a close watch, we're just friends. Just friends."

"Small steps, son," Maggie kissed his cheek and squeezed his hand, remembering all he'd suffered the past year. "Oh, Art, I'm thrilled to see you so happy and have you home, if only for a little while."

"It's good to be home, Mama."

One winter evening eight months later the February skies, dark and dreary, unleashed its vehemence. Flashes of lightening sizzled across the sky followed by earsplitting claps of thunder. The wind blew rain side-ways. The downpour pelted the windowpanes, shaking the glass.

Franklin placed two logs on the dying fire and slid the grate across the fireplace's opening. The hissing sound from the wet wood and its white smoke wafted upward. The dying flame, swaying underneath, ignited, embracing the existing flame and grew stronger. The fire roared as its blaze grew hotter. Standing at a safe distance, Franklin rubbed his hands together, feeling the warmth.

Maggie entered the study and edged next to Franklin. She slipped her arm around his waist. Peaches plodded through the door and headed to her favorite rug. The dog turned around and around and around. Finally settling on the perfect spot, she lowered herself and rested her head on her paws.

"Are the girls asleep?" Franklin asked, slipping his arm around his wife.

"Yes, I'm surprised they can sleep in this dreadful storm, but I'm thankful they can. Clayton and Paddy pulled a quilt from their bed and draped it over two chairs. They're huddled underneath telling ghost stories."

"Those boys," Franklin laughed.

A boom of thunder, crashing directly overhead, caused Maggie to jump. Willie and Tip slipped unnoticed into the room. Willie stretched out on the leather sofa. He yanked a blanket off its back and spread the cover over him. He leaned back against the sofa pillow as Tip jumped up on him. The dog crawled underneath the blanket and nestled between Willie's legs. Willie, feeling warm and cozy, closed his eyes and started to doze. Suddenly, Tip sprang from under the blanket and paced about the room. After a few minutes, he charged through the study's doorway and began to bark.

"Oh, my, that dog hates storms as much as I do," Maggie laughed. Peaches opened her eyes and sniffed. Unperturbed, she resumed her pose and went back to sleep.

"Tip!" Willie called, chasing the dog into the foyer. "Come here!"

The dog's barking increased as he neared the entrance hall by the front door. The hair on his back stood up as he began to growl and crouch lower to the floor.

"Tip!" Willie called again. "It's just rain, boy!" Watching Tip slink closer to the door, he listened more intently. "Wait! That's not rain. Someone is pounding on the door! Papa?"

Willie ran back to the study. "Papa, someone's at the door!"

"In this weather, Franklin?" Maggie asked, distressfully.

Franklin patted Maggie's arm and followed Willie to the entrance hall. A man's silhouette appeared through the stained-glass panels as lightening lit up the sky. Franklin opened the door slightly. The wind blew rain across the porch; the rocking chairs rocked madly with each gust of wind.

"Yes?" Franklin asked. "Do you need help?"

The man's coat collar was pulled up. His hat was pulled low over his face making recognition impossible. Rain pelted him unmercifully. Tip continued to bark.

"Stop!" Willie commanded, grabbing the dog by the scruff of his neck, pulling him to one side. Tip sat at his master's feet but eyed the man suspiciously.

The man cleared his throat, "Sir, it's me. Alan Woods."

Franklin invited the young man inside. Alan stepped inside the entrance hall and glanced toward the main stairs. The rain from his boots and coat puddled the floor.

"Willie, get your mother," Franklin said.

Maggie charged out of the study with Willie following close behind. "Oh my, Alan, you are drenched! It's such a miserable night to be out! Here, give me your coat and hat. Come in where it's warm."

Maggie hung the hat in the hall. She followed the men into the study. She wrapped the rain-soaked overcoat over a straight-back chair and scooted it nearer the fireplace.

"So, Alan, what on earth brings you out in this terrible storm? Here, have a seat by the fire," Franklin swung a chair around closer to the fireplace.

Alan sat in the chair, his back to the fire and began to shiver.

"Willie, give Alan that blanket while I make a pot of coffee," Maggie pointed at the sofa and hurried to the kitchen.

Maggie returned several minutes later with a cup of coffee and a large slice of bread left over from supper. She handed Alan the cup and saucer. He accepted it gratefully and sipped the warm liquid. He took a large bite out of the bread and chewed eagerly. Franklin, Maggie, and Willie, intrigued by his presence, watched Alan curiously.

"Thank you. I wasn't sure you'd let me in. I've been driving all day. The storm hit just outside of Waco." Alan took another bite of bread and swallowed. Looking at Franklin, he said, "Sir, I've come to see Claudia. Will you allow me to speak to her?"

Franklin and Maggie exchanged glances as they sat together on the sofa. Willie, feeling sorry for Alan's unawareness, leaned against the desk. Franklin took Maggie's hand.

"Alan, Claudia is not here," Franklin explained.

Alan stood to his feet. The blanket slid from his shoulders and fell in a heap onto the floor. "What? What happened? Where is she?"

"She's okay. Sit down, son," Franklin waited for Alan to be seated. "She's living with her brother in Beaumont."

Alan rubbed his hands over his face and pushed the fallen strand of hair from his forehead. Relief emerged over his face. His hands were shaking. Maggie took the empty cup and saucer from him and placed them on Franklin's desk. She returned to her place beside Franklin. Alan looked at them, tears wedged in his eyes.

"I was such a fool and a downright coward! I should have never left her…not the way I did…no note or explanation, nothing. I was…I wasn't ready to be married much less be a father! The thought scared me! Paralyzed me! I was too young but then so was she! Before I left, I told Ernie I had a better job. An outright lie. I drove from town to town looking for work. Found a small job in Abilene, but the pay hardly covered rent at the boarding house. I tried to escape, to leave everything behind. Eventually, I went home."

"Where's home, son?"

"Childress. I helped my pa pick and gin his cotton. I tried to forget about her, about Claudia. Tried to erase her from my head, but I couldn't. The more I tried to push her memory aside, the more I thought about her. I couldn't sleep and hardly ate." Alan leaned slightly, resting his elbows on his knees. "I finally told my parents. My pa said guilt was eating me alive and I should do the right thing." Alan sat upright. "That's why I'm here, sir. I want to, need to do the right thing by her. I've been such a heel!"

"We all make mistakes. Making amends is the brave and right thing to do," Franklin encouraged.

"Think she'll talk to me after what I've done to her?"

"Only Claudia can answer that. She's living with her brother, Gavin Hill. Gavin works at the Spindletop Oilfield. Find Spindletop, you'll find Gavin."

Maggie wiped empathetic tears from her cheeks. "Why don't you stay the night and make plans when you're fresh in the morning? I will bring some dry clothes for you to sleep in."

"Thank you, ma'am. Don't want to impose. I'll sleep here on the couch."

"Wouldn't you rather sleep in a comfortable bed?" Maggie offered.

"No, thank you, ma'am. This is better than the bed of my truck. You've been so kind."

Everyone settled down for the night. The storm lessened its intensity during the early morning hours and finally subsided sometime near sunrise. As Willie came down the stairs to let Tip out for the morning, Alan stood in the foyer, hat in hand, coat over his arm. Tip, deciding this guy wasn't harmful, approached, tail wagging. Alan rubbed the dog's head.

"You leaving?" Willie asked.

"Yeah, please tell your parents goodbye for me. I appreciate all they've done."

Alan turned and put on his coat and hat. Tip darted outside as soon the door was slightly cracked. Willie followed Alan to his truck. Small tree twigs and oak leaves, remanences from the storm, were scattered over the truck's hood. Alan got into the truck and slid behind the steering wheel. After starting the engine, he rolled down the window and waved. Slowly, he steered down the driveway.

"Wait!" Willie shouted.

Alan stomped on the brake as Willie ran up to the window.

"The baby is a boy. Claudia named him Matthew Alan."

Willie and Tip stood on the driveway watching the Chevy Roadster speed away.

PRIORITIES AND PROMISES

SPRING 1932

With every Spring comes the anticipation of warmer days and new life, budding trees, and blooming flowers. The coral honeysuckle vines which snaked around the porch railings had months before replaced its brown leaves for bright green. Its two-inch long coral blooms hung in clusters displaying its lovely trumpet-shaped petals and sweet scent. The fruit trees in the orchard were a slate of pastel colors. The crabapple and peach trees donned pink blossoms while the pear boasted white. Spring brings new hope and new birth.

The Spring of 1932 did not disappoint.

Peg Moore hurried into the kitchen unannounced. Her two-piece green plaid suit, long sleeve jacket over a belted matching straight skirt, seemed crumpled from her train ride from Galveston. Partially hidden under a brown felt hat, her dark hair, was pulled up in a bun. A short green feather affixed to dark green grosgrain ribbon adorned the hat.

Maggie, knowing she was coming, poured two cups of coffee. Peg joined her at the table. Smiling weakly, Peg removed her black gloves and placed them, as well as her clutch bag, to one side.

"You sounded troubled when you called from the station. Is everything okay with the baby?" Maggie asked. "I still can't believe we are grandmothers!"

Peg smiled brightly. "Yes, Jonathan is beautiful. Tiny and healthy. Perfect. Has ten fingers and ten toes and a button of a nose." She laughed. "Johnathan…oh, I forget John wants us to call him by his middle name. Edward is wonderful. John is such a doting father. You must be so proud. It's Emily who has me concerned."

"Some women do have trouble adjusting after childbirth, Peg. John hasn't mentioned anything."

"I'm sure. Daughters reveal more to their mothers than sons do. Too much sometimes, I'm afraid. Emily was so upset during her entire term. Angry at John. And angrier with herself for being unguarded and careless. Something about too much champagne and losing control while celebrating the completion of her basic studies," Peg adjusted the bow on her blouse before sipping her coffee.

Maggie thought Peg measured her words carefully and wanted to share more. But was grateful Peg did not. She was also relieved John did not share intimate details with his mother.

Peg continued, "She didn't want children for five or six more years. I'm not sure she even wanted children then. Being a doctor consumes her every thought to the point she has no time for anything or anyone else. She has struggled so being one of so few women in her classes. Has worked harder than the men just to be accepted or recognized by them. In fact, she slightly bound her body not wanting her peers or professors to know her condition. And fortunately, the dresses she wore gathered loosely below her hip. Of course, the mandatory jackets easily covered her midriff. I'm saddened this miraculous time in her life seemed so burdensome to her. Bessie has been a Godsend for sure. Without hers and John's care, our poor baby would have no one."

Peg's voice broke and she stifled back tears. "I'm so disappointed in my daughter. She's also chosen not to breastfeed. I can't imagine any mother choosing not to…I fed my mine as I know you did yours. There's such a bond there. But Emily claims I'm old-fashioned and she has no time for such things. So, Bessie sterilizes glass bottles and prepares the Nestlé formula. She and John take turns with the feedings. Emily is too busy with her last year of clinicals to be bothered! She only took two weeks from classes after Edward was born telling her professor she had laryngitis or some such nonsense."

"She's so fearful of not being accepted for an internship at John Sealy Hospital. She's so inspired by Edith Bonnet. Did you know Edith Bonnet and Frances Vanzant were at first denied internship to John Sealy simply because they were women? They appealed to Ma Ferguson, our governor at the time, and the legislature ruled women must be admitted if they're eligible. Bonnet and Vanzant were the first two women to intern at John Sealy and that was only six years ago."

"No. I didn't know. Such courageous women," Maggie sipped her coffee.

Peg continued, "Emily told me having that baby; that's what she called him, 'that baby,' was a mistake and inconvenience. She said, 'Now John has his baby. I'll not have any more!' Her defiance is so troubling…just makes me want to cry!"

Maggie reached across the table and squeezed Peg's hand. "John reports Edward is gaining weight and is quite healthy. He is beyond elated to be a father. I'm sorry Emily feels as she does. I pray she'll change her mind once her clinicals are finished. I'm happy, too, Bessie decided to stay to help. She's such a nurturing woman."

"Oh, how I wish Emily were!"

The twins burst through the mudroom giggling and jabbering. Tia followed carrying a basket of cut flowers. The girls wore matching light blue denim overalls and red checked shirts. Their hair was pulled back with dark blue ribbons.

"Hello, Mrs. Moore," Tia greeted as she placed the basket on the worktable. "Welcome home."

"Thank you, Tia. I must say, Maggie, I can't believe how much these girls have grown in just the four weeks I've been away."

Loraine ran to her mother. She pushed against Maggie's legs, subtly demanding to be lifted. Maggie raised her four-year-old to her lap. Loraine quickly scooped the remaining cookie from her mother's dessert plate. She stuffed it into her mouth and grinned like a Cheshire cat. Peg smiled, amused.

Lucy climbed upon the stepstool kept in front of the worktable and helped Tia remove the flowers from the basket. Tia took down three glass vases from the cabinet and began arranging the yellow daffodils, pink tulips, and lilac hyacinths.

"How's my Rachel?" Tia asked. "You know she's special to me."

"Oh, Rachel is doing well at the San Antonio Gazette office. Loves her position there. Working summers with her father certainly groomed her for the typing pool. She hopes one day to be a reporter if that's possible. For now, she's satisfied. She gets terribly homesick living alone in the boarding house. She is meeting new people and making friends. Joanna, one of her coworkers, has a brother Rachel mentions often." Peg laughed, "I don't think she realizes how often Timothy Talbert's name comes up in conversation!"

"I'm glad she's doing well," Maggie said. "Art tells me they often write."

"Please tell her hello for me. Maggie, stay and finish your visit with Mrs. Moore. I'll take the girls up. Okay, you two. It's naptime." Tia waited by the kitchen door for the twins to hug Peg goodbye.

"Trina, why are you so nervous?" Sam asked, holding her hand. They sat on the wicker swing on the front porch. "I would have thought last night's dinner with your parents would be more nerve-wracking than dinner tonight with mine."

Trina smiled, "I'm sure it was for you. Tonight, is my turn. What if they don't like me? What if they say no?"

Sam tilted her chin and kissed her. "If your parents have no objection, why should mine? Besides, you've been following me around for years. Mine should be used to you by now."

"You are horrible, Samuel James Bailey!" Trina jabbed his ribs with her elbow.

"Oh, no! Using my full name is not good. Should I feel fully reprimanded?" He tucked her hair behind her ear and kissed her ear lobe. "Love me?" he whispered.

Clayton burst through the front door. "Mama said dinner's ready! Hey! Are you two talking or doing something else?"

Sam stood, extending his hand to help Trina up. He reached out for Clayton, grabbing him around the shoulders. "What do you know about it, little brother? Who've you been spying on to learn such things?"

"Just you," Clayton pulled away, laughing as Trina's face reddened.

"Don't mind him," Sam smiled. Taking Trina's hand, he kissed the top of her knuckles, and led her to the dining room.

Maggie had just taken her seat at the far end of the table closest to the kitchen as Sam and Trina entered the room. The twins, sitting in their booster chairs, sat on either side of their mother. William and Clayton sat beside Lucy. Paddy sat next to Loraine. Two empty chairs sat at the end of the table next to Franklin.

"Trina, my dear, welcome," Franklin motioned his hand toward the unoccupied chairs.

Franklin offered grace after everyone was seated. With the final "amen" voiced, he served his plate then passed the platters and bowls one by one around the table.

The fluidity of filling plates, clinking dishes and scraping utensils did little to interrupt dinner conversation—the weather, upcoming local events and the town's news.

Trina placed a napkin in her lap. Sipping water from her stemmed glass, Trina tried avoiding Clayton's devilish smile. She wondered why he of all the Bailey children sat directly across from her. Sam gently nudged her. She had almost missed Franklin's question.

"Oh, yes, I'm sorry. I very much enjoy working with Judge Newman. Keeping his schedule and correspondence are very taxing at times. But I have learned so much about law."

"She's recently received a raise," Sam boasted.

"Well, good for you, Trina," Franklin said, enthusiastically.

"Sunday at church, I heard a couple of ladies say your parents are moving. Is that true?" Maggie asked.

"Yes," Trina spooned cooked carrots onto her plate and passed the bowl to Maggie. "They're moving to Hereford; my father was born and raised there. My grandmother is very ill. My father and my two younger brothers will run the family ranch. My mother will take care of the house and grandmother. My grandfather died when I was nine. I barely remember him. My eldest brother and his wife are staying here to run the feed store."

"Oh, I'm sorry to hear about your grandmother and your grandfather. That's such a wonderful thing your family is doing. I suppose you're moving as well?" Maggie asked as she cut Lucy's roasted chicken into smaller pieces.

Trina reached under the table for Sam's hand. He smiled at her and looked around the table. "This seems to be the appropriate time to share our plans."

Maggie and Franklin exchanged glances as Clayton smirked. William and Paddy listened, interested but somewhat confused.

Sam continued, "Trina and I have received her parents' blessings to be married. That was their condition for her staying in Oak Hill… that we marry. We are both eighteen and have great jobs, good salaries. We plan to marry Saturday morning. It's all been arranged with the Justice of the Peace at the courthouse. Trina's parents want to be there, of course, and are leaving for Hereford after lunch. We'll continue to live over the drugstore where I've been living if that's okay."

"What? Marriage?" Maggie could not control her outburst. "But, Sam, you are so young! Too young!" She looked at Franklin for support.

"Could we continue this conversation after dinner in my study?" Franklin asked, placing his butter knife at the top of his plate.

"Yes, sir, we can," Sam answered. "But our plans are made. We're not changing our minds!" Sam's voice bristled as he sat up straighter in his chair. Trina clutched his hand tightly.

"Oh, no, talking you out of this is not my intention at all, son. I just want to make sure you've thought everything through. This is a big step; a big decision you're making. A life-long commitment. But, if you love each other, want to take care of each other and grow old together, your mother and I will do all in our power to support you."

Maggie fidgeted with her napkin and lowered her eyes. Knowing her response to these two foolish young people was far from comparable to Franklin's. That much she did know. She finished the meal in silence.

Franklin stepped into his bedroom and leaned against the door frame. Maggie sat at her vanity brushing her hair. Holding one strand of brunette hair, she softly pulled a brush through its waves. Then brushed the other side.

"Franklin? How long have you been standing there?"

"Not long. You know how much I enjoy watching you brush your hair."

Maggie leaned forward to examine her face. She pushed her hair from her forehead. "Look at these little gray hairs and these wrinkles forming around my eyes! I'm getting old!"

Franklin stood behind her. He viewed her reflection in the mirror. She continued to pull and push her skin around her cheek bones. He bent to kiss her neck. "You, my dear, are only forty-two. You are far from old. You are as beautiful as when we first met."

"Oh, Franklin," she turned and slapped playfully at his hands. "We were just kids when we first met. Ernie was your best friend. As I remember you ignored me most of the time. It wasn't until the summer I turned fourteen that you even noticed me!"

"Hmmm, yes, you were indeed lovely at fourteen."

Maggie stood from the vanity and kissed his cheek. She unbuttoned and removed the housecoat she wore over her nightgown. She kicked off her slippers and got into bed, pulling up the covers.

She plumped up the pillows behind her and leaned back as Franklin undressed.

"Did Sam come back to talk with you after he took Trina home?"

"Yes," Franklin turned down the lights and slid into bed. Maggie leaned against his chest as he wrapped an arm around her. "We had a good talk. It's obvious he and Trina love each other. They've dated for two years, so I think they know what they feel for each other is real."

"But, Franklin, they're only eighteen. They couldn't possibly know what they're doing!"

Franklin pulled Maggie closer. "Would you rather we disagree with their decision knowing they'll get married anyway? Should we risk losing the relationship we have with our son? Yes, they're young, but so were we."

"But you'd at least finished college and I had completed one year."

"Maggie, you were only nineteen and I twenty-one when we married. We were but twenty and twenty-two when John was born."

"I know. I know, but they seem so much younger than we were! What if they start a family right away?"

"Then, we'll be grandparents again! That wouldn't be so bad, would it?"

"No, I guess not, but just think of what's ahead for them. The hard times with little money. Scraping by to pay bills, leaving hardly any money for anything else. The long hours and late nights of work. Then come the babies to feed and clothe."

Franklin pulled Maggie up to face him, "Maggie, I know starting out for us was challenging. But we were together and made it work. Looking back, is there anything you'd have done differently? Any day you would trade or change or give up?"

Tears rimmed Maggie's eyes. "No, I would not change a thing. I've loved you since I was fifteen. I promised when you asked me to spend the rest of my life with you that I would follow you anywhere.

That promise is as binding then as it is now. I love you, Franklin Bailey."

Franklin kissed her, "And I you."

They leaned back against their pillows, still entwined in each other's arms, and fell asleep.

CHRISTMAS 1933

December 1933

December days, unlike any other month, seem to morph at a fast pace. They hastily tumble from sunrise to sunset, sunset to sunrise. Like waves ebbing back and forth on the shore, they inch closer and closer to the new year. December smells are just as unique—Douglas fir pine trees, gingerbread, vanilla, cooked cranberries, roasted pecans and walnuts, basted turkeys, cooked ham, clove-covered oranges, and baked apples. December is abuzz with activity—church bazaars, pageants, school plays, candlelight services, choir cantatas, shopping, gift wrapping, caroling, tree and house decorating, wassail punch making, eggnog tasting. Year upon year, December preserves its traditions and carries hope for the upcoming year.

Such was Christmas 1933 for the Baileys.

"Tia! They're here!" Maggie buttoned up her coat and rushed out to the front porch.

Franklin pulled the truck to the end of the drive and stopped. William stood in the back of the truck bed and peered over the cab. Clayton and Paddy scrambled over the sides and jumped to the ground. Lucy and Loraine shimmied across the front seat and joined their brothers. Maggie pulled her coat tightly around her. Stomping her feet, she hoped to lessen the December chill. William hauled up a six-foot Douglas fir and pushed it forward. Clayton, a strapping young lad of twelve, heaved the tree onto his shoulder. Paddy, now eleven, balanced the other end. They carried the tree between them toward the house.

"Look! Mama! Look!" Lucy cried, skipping excitedly behind them. Her curly hair, as if mocking the excitement, bounced with her every move.

Franklin and William retrieved a second tree, ten feet in length, and followed Loraine and the others. A parade of Christmas cheer entered the house.

"Oh, Franklin, these are perfect. Boys, take that one to the study. The stand is already in place. The bigger one goes here." Maggie stood in the center of the foyer next to the stairs.

"Girls, your coats, please." Lucy and Loraine, fidgeted and wiggled as Maggie pulled off their coats and draped them over her arm.

Lucy hastily removed her pink mittens. She dropped one but scooped it quickly from the floor and handed it to her mother. Loraine pulled her woolen cap from her head and held it up for her mother to retrieve. The girls stood together and giggled with excitement.

Franklin and William propped the tree in the stand. One of the many pinecones clinging to the lower branches, loosened by the jolt, fell off. It rolled onto the floor and finally rested against William's boots. William scooted the cone to one side with the toe of his boot as he held the tree steady.

"More to the right, I think," Franklin observed, removing his coat.

William adjusted the tree, screwed the three prongs into place and stood up. Cocking his head side-to-side, he judged for himself the correct positioning of the tree. It was perfect. He took a deep breath, filling his lungs with the pungent smell of pine. Loraine and Lucy clapped their hands happily and dashed into the study to check the progress there.

"Oh, these were in the mailbox," Franklin waited for Maggie to hang the coats by the front door, then handed her a stack of mail.

"How were the Nelsons?" Maggie asked. "Who would have ever guessed a tree farm could be so profitable? This Douglas fir is beautiful."

"We would have been home sooner. The girls started a game of tag running between the rows of trees. Time slipped away. Mrs. Nelson, as always, had hot cocoa for us. She said to tell you hello."

"How nice. Lovely couple. I'll look for her at the Christmas Eve service. William, would you bring down the boxes of decorations in the loft, please?" Maggie asked.

"Come check the little tree, Papa," Lucy pulled at Franklin, coaxing him to the study.

"Franklin, ask Clayton and Paddy to bring in the wreaths from the kitchen on the worktable. Tia and I made them for the doorways. I'll tell them where they should be hung."

Maggie stepped down into the parlor and sat on the brocade wing-back chair facing the windows. She placed the envelopes in her lap, sorting them. One address immediately caught her attention. She ripped opened the envelope. Franklin stepped up next to her chair and awaited further instructions.

"Franklin! Art is coming home!" She flapped the letter in the air. "Oh, this will be the first Christmas we've all been together in four years! Do you think Art has finally made amends with John and Emily?"

Franklin sat on the arm of the chair, patting her shoulder. "Would be our Christmas miracle, wouldn't it?"

"And here's a card from Claudia. Isn't it pretty?" Maggie turned the card where Franklin could see a painting of shepherds guarding sheep on a hill. "I love Hall Brothers cards. They're always so pretty. Hall Brothers or Hallmark, which is it?"

"They've changed their name to Hallmark, I believe."

"Of course, oh, there's a letter folded inside."

Maggie unfolded the paper and read aloud.

"Family, greetings, and Merry Christmas from Beaumont. We are well and hope you are the same. Alan is doing so well at Spindletop. We

were both surprised he traded construction for oil. But he likes the work. Although dirty and grimy, it pays well. We have saved enough money to buy a house. Matthew is growing, running everywhere. At two, he's quite the chatter box. We are sorry, too, to miss being with you again this year. Mom and Dad are coming here for Christmas, so we are looking forward to that. Susan, Gavin, and Cora send their best. I'm sending a separate card and letter to your address for Granma. I'll write again soon when I have more time.

Much love and Merry Christmas,

Alan, Claudia, and Matthew Woods"

Maggie smiled, "Bless her. She signs her married name as if we wouldn't know who she was without it! She's so happy!"

"Hello? Anybody home?" a voice called from the vestibule.

"It's Trina and Sam!" Franklin exclaimed.

"You're not starting without us, are you?" Trina asked, stepping into the foyer.

Sam removed her coat and hung it along with his on pegs by the front door.

"Trina, my dear," Maggie kissed her cheek. "You look lovely. New dress?"

Trina, her face aglow, self-consciously touched her stomach and nodded. She wore a sky-blue and light pink floral chiffon dress with long flowing sleeves that rested at her wrists. The straight-lined shift had evenly spaced knife-pleats extending from the scooped neck to the hem. The pastel colors complimented her blonde hair and blue eyes.

Sam kissed his mother's cheek. "Okay, where do we start? Shall I bring in the ladders?"

"Yes, there's so much to do. If we divide and conquer, I think we can have the trees and house decorated before John and Emily and Granma arrive tomorrow."

"They'll miss all the fun!" Franklin exclaimed with a chuckle.

"Maggie, the house looks beautiful! The candles, wreaths, garlands, and ribbons. I see some of the glass ornaments I gave you are on the tree," Bessie said, slipping her arm through Maggie's. "Thank you for letting me nap. The drive was long, but I'm relieved Edward slept most of the way."

"Thank you, we had fun decorating. Franklin tells us every year, as if we could ever forget, those ornaments were his as a child. Come join us in the music room. The girls are reenacting their parts from the Christmas play. They were angels."

Bessie laughed, "Of course, what else could they be?"

The Baileys sat around the room awaiting the entrance of the performers. Bessie took her seat next to Franklin on the sofa. William stood behind them. Clayton and Paddy sat cross-legged on the floor. Sam and Trina sat in the wingback chairs near the windows while John and Emily sat nearest the piano. Edward sat happily on John's knee. Peaches and Tip, also members of the Bailey family, curled up next to the boys.

Maggie played an introduction on the piano. Tia followed Lucy and Loraine into the room, then hurried to stand beside William.

"Santos coming?" William whispered to Tia.

"The girls performed for him yesterday," Tia patted his arm and smiled.

The twins wore long-sleeved white muslin dresses that touched the tops of their bare feet. Their wings, white lace stretched over wire, arched over their heads. Tied with a bow in the back, the wings, fastened over their shoulders and under their arms. Wreaths of white flowers perched around their foreheads. Maggie smiled and began to play.

Lucy and Loraine—completely uninhibited by age, having celebrated their sixth birthday a mere day before—held hands. With big smiles on their faces, they swayed back and forth as they sang two Christmas carols.

With the last verse sung, they curtsied and bowed. Applause and cheers erupted causing Lucy's face to beam. Loraine ran to Franklin's outstretched arms.

Tia hurried back toward the kitchen and announced. "Cookies and desserts are served in the dining room."

Clayton, Paddy and William, typical hungry boys, did not require a second invitation nor hesitate at the first one. They scrambled from the room followed by their dogs and raced to be the first to fill their plates. Desserts of all sorts—sugar cut-outs, date roll ups, cranberry walnut balls, and cinnamon crescent cookies, plus apple, cherry, and pecan pies.

Edward began to whine and fuss. Emily's eyes darted alarmingly toward John. "It's been a long day," John said, lifting Edward to his hip. "I'll put him to bed and then join you."

Maggie reached out for her grandson. "Nonsense. Enjoy the desserts and visit with the family. I'll take him up. It's not often I have the pleasure of putting my grandson to bed. Come here, big boy." Maggie secured the twenty-month-old baby on her hip. Edward's giggles could be heard echoing down the hall.

Franklin and Bessie led the twins to the dining room or more precisely, the girls pulled and tugged at them. "Hurry!" they exclaimed in unison.

Sam patted Trina's knee, "Shall I bring you a plate with some of everything?"

Trina smiled and nodded as Emily said, "John, that sounds nice. I'll talk to Trina while you fill our plates."

After their husbands left the room, Emily visibly examined Trina as a doctor might observe a patient, checking for skin disorders or imperfections of some kind.

"So, Sam told us congratulations are in order. When are you due?"

"Yes, thank you, in May." Trina bubbled with excitement.

"I've never figured out why women are congratulated. There's nothing rewarding about getting fat, your stomach bulging out embarrassingly under your clothes. And then your feet swell into a bigger shoe size. Your firm youthful bodies are completely lost. I hated the whole thing!" Emily exclaimed.

"Don't be surprised if Sam fawns over you and dotes on you like you're a piece of glass, completely helpless. Then after the baby comes, you're no longer considered frail or delicate. Once again, you're expected to wait on your husband and keep him happy. Your life will never be the same! But I refuse to let a baby change mine! Don't you work at the courthouse?"

Trina, clearly embarrassed, answered, "Yes, I do."

"I hope you continue to do so. How long must we women let some man—father, husband, or otherwise—decide when and where and how long we can work? Don't be brainwashed either by old wives' tales about a woman's job is solely to cook and clean. And your only purpose is to have a baby every year or two! That's definitely not for me!"

When Sam entered carrying two dessert plates, Emily stood, "Think I'll go help John fix my plate. I've missed Tia's cookies."

Trina took the plate Sam offered and placed it on her lap. He sat next to her and took a big bite of pecan pie.

"Hmm, Tia did it again." Noticing she was not eating; he touched her arm. "Trina, are you okay?"

Tears welled in her eyes, "Sam, will you love me when I'm fat?"

"What? Where did that come from? Sweetheart, we're having a baby. And from all I know about that, your body does change." He chuckled slightly and slipped an arm around her shoulders.

"You won't be fat! You'll be carrying a baby, our baby, right here." He gently stroked Trina's stomach. "This little one is a miracle, and I am so thrilled. That's all that matters to me. You and our baby."

Trina kissed him, "Promise you'll always love me."

Sam looked perplexed, "You don't need to ask. I love you more than anything in this world! Now, feed our baby some of that delicious apple pie."

Maggie, legs curled underneath her, sat in the parlor on the sofa. A yellow and white crocheted blanket was draped about her shoulders. She blew softly across the steam drifting from her coffee cup. The house was dark. Its occupants were finally settled and quiet. She admired the festive view of the foyer and stairs. The ten-foot tree was adorned with glistening silver garland and pinecones and bright red bows. At sunrise, in seven brief hours, sunrays would spill from the stained-glass oval window at the top of the stairs. The ornaments would come alive dancing in sparkling prisms of color.

Wrapped packages of red, green, gold and silver lay beneath the tree. Sprigs of pine branches adorned door frames. Pine branches, tied together forming garlands, wrapped around the stair railings. Eight big red bows, evenly spaced, were secured to the handrails. Mistletoe suspended with a red ribbon hung from every doorway. Maggie's treasured ceramic nativity pieces Franklin had given her their first Christmas was displayed on the small table in the front of her.

Maggie smiled.

Oh, you're smiling. Are you thinking what I'm thinking? Are you remembering past Christmases? You know, I remember all fifteen of them. Every year I looked forward to watching the children open their gifts and play with their toys. Such gaiety and pure excitement!

My favorite one though was the year Willie was old enough to read the Christmas story from the Bible. Oh, I know he's older now and prefers to be called William, but that's the Christmas I'll never forget. How I loved hearing the story about Joseph and Mary and baby Jesus. And about the angels singing from the heavens proclaiming great joy. And the part about a bright star leading the shepherds to the place Jesus was born. I can't imagine a star that bright! The Texas sky holds zillions of stars but not one has ever shone as brightly as that one did that night over Bethlehem. What a glorious night it must have been!

Maggie snuggled under the blanket and whispered, "Tomorrow is Christmas Eve."

"The Christmas tablecloth has been pressed, Maggie. Where are the red candles? I'll finish setting the dining room table for lunch," Bessie held the red tablecloth draped over both forearms to prevent wrinkles.

"Thank you. The candles are in the pantry. Patrick Thomas! Stop that!" Maggie swatted at Paddy's hands as he swiped three pieces of crisp bacon from the platter on the worktable. He crammed them in his mouth and grinned.

"Go tell your father breakfast is ready. We're eating in here. Girls, have you washed your hands?"

Lucy and Loraine jumped down from their chairs at the kitchen table and rushed to the mudroom to wash up. Racing back to the table, they heard John coming down the back stairs. He walked into the kitchen carrying Edward.

"Eddie!" Loraine exclaimed, tickling her nephew's legs. "Put his chair by me!"

John obeyed his little sister's wishes, placing Edward's highchair near her chair.

"Emily won't be joining us for breakfast, Mama. She wanted to sleep."

"Hmm, something smells good," Franklin entered the kitchen followed closely by Clayton, Paddy and Bessie.

William hurried down the back stairs. "Did I miss the cinnamon rolls?"

Maggie placed the warm platters of cinnamon rolls, baked apples, bacon, sausage patties, and scrambled eggs on the table. "Take your seats. Franklin, offer thanks, please."

Maggie sat down, placed a napkin in her lap and bowed her head.

"Heavenly Father, Creator of all things, thank You for this food and for our many blessings and provisions. Thank You for this Christmas season as we are reminded of Your love and Your Son's birth. Be with us this day as we celebrate together for the first time in several years. Fill us with Your love, grace and mercy. Amen," Franklin prayed.

"Boys, there are enough rolls for you to have two," Maggie began. "Eat quickly; we have a busy day! Lucy, wipe your mouth with your napkin, please."

"What time are Sam and Trina picking up Art from the station?" Bessie asked.

"10:00 a.m., I believe," Franklin answered, spooning a baked apple onto his plate.

"After you've finished eating, and this applies to everyone, go upstairs and change into your church clothes. Granma and I will help the girls. We'll be leaving at 11:00 a.m. to go to Randall's Photography," Maggie instructed. "Mr. Randall was so kind to open his studio on Christmas Eve to take our portrait."

"After hearing Art and John would both be in town, he willingly agreed. He knew this was a special occasion for our family," Franklin added, winking at John.

John smiled and offered Edward another bite of scrambled eggs.

"After that is done, we will come home and have lunch at 2:00 p.m. with Ernie's family and the Moores. We'll exchange gifts. Then have desserts and eggnog before going to church at 8:00 p.m. for the candlelight service. Our family gift exchange will be in the morning," Maggie continued.

"When Santa comes?" Loraine asked excitedly causing Lucy to giggle.

"Yes," Maggie laughed. "Any questions?"

Franklin chuckled before gulping down his last swig of coffee, "You've shared today's schedule with us all week, my dear. But I may be a bit unclear. What time is lunch today?"

Casting a frown at her husband, everyone sensed Maggie's schedule was no joking matter. Franklin stood, pushed his chair from the table and carried his plate and utensils to the sink. The others followed and then proceeded quickly upstairs to dress.

Tia entered the back door. "I'm here!"

"Delores, happy Christmas Eve!"

Tia tied an apron around her waist as Maggie kissed her cheek.

"Go on, now. I'll clean the kitchen. Thank you for suggesting Luis and I have breakfast together. Art will be here soon. Go!" Tia shooed at Maggie with the end of her apron.

Maggie stood in front of her full-length mirror examining the dress she had chosen for the day. The dress, a black and white floral, was not new, but was her best. Maggie adjusted the white collar that overlapped across the bodice. She buttoned the front quickly and buckled the belt. She smoothed the form-fitting skirt that flared slightly ten inches above her black pumps. She ran her fingers across a wave that was coming undone and pushed the hair pin back in place. She slipped on her favorite pearl earrings, glanced again in the mirror, then hurried to her daughters' room.

"Be still. Arms up," Bessie urged as she pulled Loraine's dress over her head.

"Ouch! Granma! That hurts!"

"I'm sorry, sweetie," Bessie kissed the crying girl's arm. "We accidentally left a straight pin in the hem."

Maggie took Lucy's dress from the bed and checked for any undetected pins hidden in the garment. Lucy stood still, but apprehensively, as Maggie lifted the dress over her head. Once dressed, the two girls stood together for inspection.

"You are lovely indeed," Maggie proudly observed. Bessie nodded and smiled.

The girls wiggled about, swishing their skirts. The dresses were white taffeta with sheer puffy sleeves and an overskirt of white voile. The front bodices were smocked. Loraine's dress had a green plaid sash, Lucy's red. They wore matching red ribbons to hold their curls. Both girls wore white stockings and white paten shoes.

As Maggie asked the girls to turn around for one final review, William knocked on the door. Sam's car was pulling into the driveway. The girls squealed, jumping up and down.

"That's how I feel," Maggie whispered to Bessie. They led the twins from their bedroom toward the main stairs.

As Maggie looked over the railing, she saw Sam, Art, and Franklin standing in the foyer. As they neared the bottom steps, Loraine pulled free from Maggie's hold, and ran down the last few steps. She skipped across the wood floor and flew into Art's outstretched arms.

"Hey, there, little girl!" Art twirled her around.

As soon as he put Loraine down, Lucy grabbed him. He spun Lucy around then knelt on one knee and hugged his sisters tightly. "You've grown so much! You will always be my little Christmas angels."

Art stood to hug his mother and grandmother.

"Excuse me," Sam said. "I'll just step outside; don't know what's keeping Trina and the boys."

"We'll go out with you. I should bring in my own bags." Art clapped William's back.

Bessie grabbed the girls before they followed their brothers outside.

Franklin moved toward Maggie and kissed her on the cheek. "You are enchanting."

When he kissed her mouth, he pointed across the room to the mistletoe hanging over the doorway in the vestibule. "You're supposed to be standing under the mistletoe when kissed," Maggie laughed, readjusting her hair.

"Close enough," Franklin smiled.

Grinning, Clayton and Paddy entered the foyer and stood next to their mother. Trina and Sam followed and slipped in beside Bessie.

Maggie looked at her sons' sheepish faces; each behaving as if she'd caught him with a hand in the cookie jar. "What's going on?"

Paddy looked toward the door and Maggie's eyes followed his gaze. Art stood in the hallway by the front door and extended his hand. A young woman dressed in a light green wool suit and a matching green hat was led across the floor. The couple stopped in front of the waiting family.

"Family, it's my honor to present Miss Rosa De Leon, my fiancée."

Maggie rushed toward the girl, kissing her cheek, "Rosa, how lovely to meet you! Welcome to our home and to our family!"

"Yes, welcome!" Franklin kissed her cheek. "Merry Christmas!"

Rosa smiled, "Hello, it's so nice to finally meet you. Art speaks of you often. I feel like I already know you."

"I guess you've met Art's younger brothers?" Franklin asked, laughing.

Clayton and Paddy, standing like stone statues a few feet in front of her, stared.

Rosa smiled, "Yes, I have."

William entered carrying three suitcases, balanced precariously under his arms. He eased them onto the floor. He clapped Art on the back and whispered, "Her eyes do look like pools of dark honey, big brother."

Art swung playfully at William and then took his place beside Rosa. He glanced at her. Rosa stood confidently and poised. Her green felt hat, tilted to one side, covered most of her hair swept underneath. Her exposed hair was as dark as molasses. Her skin was smooth and the color of creamy milk chocolate. Rosa glimpsed at Art and smiled. Charmed by her amber eyes and long, dark lashes, he smiled back.

Rosa moved toward the girls. Leaning slightly, she placed her hands on her knees. "Let's see. You must be Loraine and you're Lucy, right?"

The girls giggled in response. "You both are just as beautiful as Art described. We brought birthday presents for you. Sorry we missed your party." Lucy and Loraine grinned brightly and grabbed Rosa's hands.

Tia came bounding down the hall wiping her hands on her apron. The twins stood between Art and Rosa. Lucy held Art's hand, Loraine Rosa's. Tia hurried toward Art and hugged him tightly. She then pushed past him to kiss Rosa's cheeks.

"You must be our Rosa!" Tia exclaimed.

"Who's Rosa?" A voice sounded from the stairway. Everyone turned to see John escorting Bessie down the stairs. As they approached the visitor, Maggie pulled the girls to one side to stand by her. Franklin took the liberties to introduce them.

John and Art exchanged hugs. "Congratulations, Art!" John clapped his brother's back, then shook Rosa's hand. "Welcome, Rosa. So nice to meet you."

Bessie took Rosa's hands, "Welcome to our family, my dear. You are as lovely as Art described. Maybe even more so. Please, call me Granma."

"Do we have time, Maggie, to sit in the study and get more comfortable? Rosa must be weary from travel. It's not that far to Randall's...." Franklin stopped mid-sentence as an eerie silence masked the room.

Franklin glanced at Art who was staring up at the top of the stairs. Emily stood on the landing, frozen in place like an ice sculpture. John rushed forward and waited for his wife at the bottom of the stairs. Rosa, upon seeing Emily, reached out for Art's hand.

The pine garlands and red ribbons served as Emily's runway as she slowly made her descent. Everyone's eyes were still drawn on her. She looked stunning in an almond-colored crepe dress covered in lace. Its large collar easily served as a shawl wrapping around her arms exposing her shoulders and neck. The dress draped tightly around her bodice and hips, flattering her figure. Soft flowing pleats flared below her knees. Her almond-colored shoes matched her dress as well as the wide-brimmed hat and bag she carried in her hand. Her copper hair was pulled up off her neck and rolled into a bun on one side. The tops and sides of her hair were covered in finger waves. A double strand of white pearls with a floral shaped diamond pendant at its center sat perfectly about her neck.

As she stepped into the foyer, she took John's arm. "My! What's going on down here?"

Proudly, John escorted her across the floor and stopped in front of Art and Rosa.

"Emmy, this is Rosa De Leon, Art's fiancée."

"Hello," Emily said briskly without extending a hand.

She then turned her full attention on Art. She stared, studying him thoroughly. In a cynical voice, she said, "Funny thing, I really expected to see you wearing smelly chaps, manure covered boots, jingly spurs and a big sombrero!"

Rosa clutched Art's arm and stepped closer. Art's jaw muscles tightened.

"And I expected you in a long, starched white coat wearing a stethoscope around your neck instead of those expensive pearls."

John laughed trying to ease the mood, "She's almost there, Art. She's been accepted to an internship at the Sacramento Memorial Hospital. We leave for California in February. I'll be heading up a drugstore warehouse there beginning in March. Granma is staying here, though. California is too far away from Texas for her liking."

Emily kept eye contact with Art, piercing him with her stare, daring him to be the first to look away. Then she turned her eyes squarely on Rosa. "You should have Art bring you to California one day to see the giant redwoods. I'm sure it gets quite dull and monotonous for you. With your only scenery being squat mesquite trees, scraggly sage, flat horizons, and the back ends of horses. You probably feel completely out of touch way down there on the tip of Texas!"

With clinched jaws, Art interjected, "You don't know what you're talking about! The sunrises and sunsets have nothing to obstruct your view. Some of the prettiest I've ever seen. The stars are breathtaking; the constellations easily seen. Texas sage is covered in lavender blooms after a rain. Nothing compares to living in South Texas."

Emily laughed and squeezed John's arm, "Oh, my, still so competitive. John, be a dear and get Eddie. He's dressed and in his crib. I didn't want to carry him and wrinkle my dress."

John kissed her hand and bounded up the steps two at a time to retrieve his baby boy. Art analyzed Emily as she turned her back to talk to Maggie, Trina, and Granma. She was beautiful still—burnt copper hair, fair skin, startling blue eyes, a perfect figure. There was something noticeably different about her, something amiss—her inner beauty had faded. It was completely gone.

Franklin pulled the chain from his vest pocket and checked the time on his watch. "Maggie, hon, we're behind schedule! We must be going."

"William, your vest and jacket," Maggie pointed at her son.

William looked down at his attire—white shirt, red bow tie, red suspenders, cuffed black trousers, and black dress shoes. William hurried upstairs to retrieve his suit vest and jacket as his mother inspected his younger brothers.

Franklin turned, "Art, if you'd drive my car and take your mother, Granma, the girls, and Rosa, of course. John, Emily, and Eddie may ride with Trina and Sam in his car. The boys will ride with me in the pickup. Everyone knows your assignments. Grab your coats. Let's go!"

Tia wrung her hands, "Oh, I've got to get going, too! Santos should have the tamales heating on the pit. I need to check on him. Lunch will almost be ready when you return."

"Tamales?" Rosa blurted.

Art squeezed her elbow and laughed, "Yeah, tamales. We have 'em every Christmas Eve. I told you a little bit of Mexico lived in the heart of Texas!"

"Art, do you mind if I stay behind to help Tia? I want to meet Santos, too." Rosa lifted her soft amber eyes, pleadingly searching his.

Art smiled, knowing he could never begrudge her anything, "Okay, and when we get back, you'll meet the rest of the clan. I can't wait for you to meet Rachel. Tia, take good care of her."

Rosa beamed and tiptoed to kiss Art on the cheek. She and Tia locked arms as they walked down the hallway. Their heads were huddled together. Speaking softly in Spanish, Tia pushed open the kitchen door.

Maggie smiled and slipped her arm through Art's as they walked together to the front door. He leaned down and kissed her cheek when they stood under the mistletoe. She squeezed his hand before he escorted Bessie and his sisters out to Franklin's car.

Maggie reached for her coat, but Franklin took it off the rack for her. He helped her slip it on, then turned her around to face him. He pointed to the mistletoe hanging from the doorway and kissed her. "Maggie, girl, what a wonderful Christmas. Our family is here, every single one. This is a Christmas we'll always remember."

Maggie patted her husband's face and smiled. "Yes, we will! Where's William?"

"He's coming," Franklin answered.

Art came back to the house to escort his mother to the car. She smiled proudly as he took her arm. They proceeded down the porch steps to the car.

William ran down the stairs and skidded across the floor. He snatched his overcoat off the peg and hurriedly slipped it on. William and Franklin were the last two Baileys out of the house. As Franklin passed through the door; he patted the doorframe twice.

"Papa, why do you do that?" William asked.

"Do what, son?"

"Pat the doorframe as you leave the house. I've seen you do it before, but never asked."

"Oh, that, I don't know. I guess because my father always did. I remember he'd say it was just a little silent prayer thanking God for our family and our home. It just stuck with me. God has surely blessed us, William. Merry Christmas, son."

"Merry Christmas, Papa!"

Franklin grabbed his fifteen-year-old son around the shoulders. The two walked arm and arm toward the others waiting in their cars.

Oh, no! I must have fallen asleep. You didn't wake me! Are we still looking at pictures? Where is everyone? Stuart? Lizzy? Frank? Oh, I hear them on the porch. There you are!

"Well, kiddos, it's time we headed back to town," Frank announced as he sat beside Mary on the porch swing.

"Aw! Grandpa, I'm not ready to go! Can't we stay longer?" Lizzy asked.

Lizzy and Frankie were sitting on the top step of the porch. Lizzy leaned against the limestone column with her feet stretched out onto her mother's lap.

Frankie stood and pulled Lizzy to her feet. "Come on, little britches, we need to go. Stuart? Where are you?"

Stuart ran around from the side of the house. "Hey! There's a gazebo out back! Did you know that?" he exclaimed, huffing for breath.

Frank offered his hand and Mary got up from the swing. He smiled at his grandson. "Yes, Stu, we knew. It's time to go."

"We promised Sister we'd take her to Luby's for dinner," Aunt Lucy said, as Frank assisted her up from a rocking chair.

"We must not keep her waiting," Frank added.

This is always the hard part…saying goodbye. Watching them load into their cars and leave. I have watched them leave so many times I've lost count. I will miss them so much…until next time, goodbye, my dears. And I will be here waiting…for I have no other place to go.

Oh, have you not figured out who I am yet? It's really quite simple when you think about it. Why, I am the one who protected them from rain, the howling winds, the blistering heat, and the frigid winter storms. I am the very one who experienced their every joy and every defeat. I was present at the birth of each child, as they prepared for their first day of school and celebrated their graduation from college. I was here at their weddings and their funerals. I was here when times were hard and difficult and seemed almost impossible to go on. Then again, when their lives were fun and carefree eased by all sorts of new inventions and hope-filled days. I knew when they were joyful and elated. Or when they were sad and depressed and cried themselves to sleep. I heard their prayers. I knew their future schemes, their fears from the past and their deepest secrets.

For I am the roof who protected them; the walls who embraced them, the floors who supported them; the windows and doors who emitted God's glorious rays of sunlight and beams of moonlight. I am simply…their house!

Odd, did you say? You don't think a house has a story to tell? Well, the next time you are traveling down an old dusty farm road and see an old, deserted farmhouse, stop. Ask her if she has a story to tell? I feel positive she does. She just might possibly share her heart with you… oh, hers might not be a heart of Texas, like mine. But it would be her heart…her story.

GENEALOGY

Name	Birth	Relationship	Age 2005
Frank Bailey	1946	Main	59
Mary Francesca Gardner	1949	Spouse	56
Francesca (Frankie) Milton	1973	Daughter	32
Stuart Jackson Milton	1995	Grandson	10
Elizabeth (Lizzy) Milton	1999	Granddaughter	6
William Franklin Bailey	1918	Father	87
Caroline Hawkins Bailey	1922	Mother	83

Name	Birth Yr.	Relationship	Age 1918	Age 1927	Age 1930	Age 1933
Franklin Stuart Bailey	1887	Grandfather	31	40	43	46
Margaret (Maggie) Bond	1889	Grandmother	29	38	41	44
John Cameron	1909	Uncle	9	18	21	24
Emily Diane Moore	1911	Aunt	7	16	19	22
Mar. 9.2.1929						
Jonathan Edward, son	1931	Cousin				2
Arthur (Art) Tilman	1911	Uncle	7	16	19	22
Samuel James	1913	Uncle	5	14	18	20
William (Willie) Franklin	1918	Father	--	9	12	15
Clayton Stuart	1921	Uncle	--	6	9	12
Patrick (Paddy) Thomas	1922	Uncle	--	5	8	11
Lucinda Mae & Loraine Rae	1927	Aunts	--	--	3	6

Name	Birth Yr.	Relationship	Age 1918	Age 1927	Age 1930	Age 1933
Ernest Randall Bond	1887	Maggie's Brother	31	40	43	46
Suzie Douglas Bond	1901	Spouse, Div. 1918	17			
Elizabeth Foster Bond	1883	Spouse, Mar. 1921	35	44	47	50
Anne Collette Foster	1904	Stepdaughter	14	23	26	29
Dottie Gayle Foster	1908	Stepdaughter	10	19	22	25
Harold Howard Foster	1913	Stepson	5	14	17	20
Owen Randall Bond	1918	Son (Suzie Bond)	--	9	12	15
Carter Eugene Bond	1922	Son (Elizabeth)	--	5	8	11
Claude Branham Bond	1857	Father (Pops)	61	70	73	75
Alma Chilton Bond	1865	Mother (Gram)	53	62	65	68

Name	Birth Yr.	Relationship	Age 1918	Age 1927	Age 1930	Age 1933
Wilson Lawrence Hill	1882	Head	36	45	48	51
Kaye Oliver Hill	1886	Spouse, Dec. 1912				
Lorna Bailey Hill	1895	Spouse, Franklin Bailey's sister	23	32	35	38
Alexander Layton Hill	1905	Son (Kaye)	13	22	25	28
Gavin Oliver Hill	1908	Son (Kaye)	10	19	22	25
Susan Beatrice Hill	1913	Daughter	5	14	17	20
Claudia Joelle Hill	1915	Daughter	3	12	15	18

Div. - Divorced

Mar.- Married

Dec. - Deceased

BIBLIOGRAPHY

"10 Things You May Not Know About the Dust Bowl" by Christopher Klein
https://www.history.com/news/10-things-you-may-not-know-about-the-dust-bowl
Access date August18, 2021

"1920's Women's Fashion & Clothing Trends"
https://vintagedancer.com/1920s/1920s-womens-fashion/
Access date August 18, 2021

"Alice Paul (1885-1977)" National Women's History Museum
www.womenshistory.org/education-resources/biographies/alice-paul
Access date September 8, 2021

"All About Water Pumping Windmills"
https://offgridquest.com/on-the-farm/all-about-water-pumping-windmills
Access date August 18, 2021

"An Informal Look at Oak Hill History" by James Scott Bankston, 12.6.11
https://oakhillgazette.com/history/2011/12/an-informal-look-at-oak-hill-history/
Access date August 18, 2021

"Dr. Edith Marguerite Bonnet Papers - The Portal to Texas History"
https://texashistory.unt.edu/explore/collections/BONNET
Access date September 8, 2021

"Early Innovation: 1910s – 30s – Hallmark Corporate"
https://corporate.hallmark.com/about/hallmark-cards-company/history/early-innovation-1910s-30s/
Access date September 8, 2021

"How 1918 Flu Pandemic Revolutionized Public Health" by Laura Spinney
https://www.smithsonianmag.com/history/how-1918-flu-pandemic-revolutionized-public-health-180965025/
Access date September 8, 2021

"How Light Was Brought to Rural Texas"
www.smartchoicecoops.com/html/history.htm
Access date September 8, 2021

"Infant Feeding in the 20th Century: Formula and Beikost" The Journal of Nutrition Volume 131, Issue 2, February 2001, Pages 409S-420S
https//doi.org/10.1093/jn/131.2.409S ---
Access date September 8, 2021

Kyvig, David E. *Daily Life in The United States 1920-1940, How Americans Lived Through The 'Roaring Twenties' And The Great Depression.*
Rev ed. Chicago: Ivan R. Dee, 2002, 2004

"Los Kineños-King Ranch"
https://king-ranch.com/about-us/history/los-kinenos/
Access date September 8, 2021

"Oak Hill, Texas (Travis, County)"
https://www.tshaonline.org/handbook/online/entries/oak-hill-tx-travis-county
Access date September 8, 2021

"Pharmacy" by Esther Jane Wood Hall
https://www.tshaonline.org/handbook/entries/pharmacy
Access date September 8, 2021

"President Wilson on the Armistice, 17 November 1918" Source Records of the Great War, Vol VI, ed, Charles F. Horne, *National Alumni 1923*
https://firstworldwar.com/source/armistice_Wilson2.htm
Access date September 8, 2021

"Quarter Horses – King Ranch"
https://king-ranch.com/about-us/history/quarter-horses/
Access date August 18, 2021

"Spindletop-Geyser, Timeline & Discovery-HISTORY"
https://www.history.com/topics/landmarks/spindletop
Access date September 8, 2021

"SMITHVILLE, TEXAS"
https://www.tshaonline.org/handbook/entries/smithville-tx
Access date September 8, 2021

"Stock Market Crash of 1929: Black Tuesday Cause & Effects-HISTORY"
https://www.history.com/topics/great-depression/1929-stock-market-crash
Access date September 8, 2021

"The Beginning of Chevy Truck History: 1918-1928"
www.cjponyparts.com/resources/chevy-truck-history
Access date September 8, 2021

"World War I" by Katherine Kuehler Walters, updated April 1, 2021
https://www.tshaonline.org/handbook/entries/world-war-i
Access date September 8, 2021

"What Was Women's Fashion Like in the 1930s?" by Chelsea Whitaker
https://www.rebelsmarket.com/blog/posts/what-was-women-s-fashion-like-in-the-1930s.html
Access date September 8, 2021

"Women's Suffrage – The U.S. Movement, Leaders & Amendment – History"
https://www.history.com/topics/womens-history/the-fight-for-womens-suffrage
Access date September 8, 2021

AFTERWORD

The idea for this story and its characters have developed over several years from two basic avenues—history and genealogy.

I have had the privilege of touring plantations in Louisiana and mansions in Miami, Florida, and Asheville, North Carolina. Their architecture, furnishings, and landscaped gardens were breathtaking and awe-inspiring. As rich in history as those were, I am most intrigued by old, dilapidated or abandoned farmhouses. Upon seeing one I wonder who lived there, how long they lived there, and what stories the inhabitants would tell.

My parents, as well as my paternal and maternal grandparents, were reared on small farms in Texas. It's interesting to think about their lives and all they endured and experienced during the early 1900s. As a youngster, I was not that interested in their pasts. I often regret not asking more questions about how their childhood and young adult lives were different than mine. They will always be my heroes, treasure troves of perseverance and wisdom.

FAMILY PHOTO 1910

FAMILY PHOTO 1921

FAMILY PHOTO 1930

FAMILY PHOTO 1936

FAMILY PHOTO 1936

Printed in the United States
by Baker & Taylor Publisher Services